Hot SEAL,
Tijuana Nights

SEALs in Paradise

CAT JOHNSON

New York Times & USA Today Bestselling Author

ISBN: 9781095469514

ALSO BY CAT JOHNSON

HOT SEALS

Night with a SEAL
Saved by a SEAL
SEALed at Midnight
Kissed by a SEAL
Protected by a SEAL
Loved by a SEAL
Tempted by a SEAL
Wed to a SEAL
Romanced by a SEAL
Rescued by a Hot SEAL
Betting on a Hot SEAL
Escape with a Hot SEAL
Matched with a Hot SEAL
SEAL the Deal
Hot SEAL in Hollywood

CHAPTER ONE

Zach closed his eyes to fully appreciate the water pounding hard and hot on the muscles still sore from Hell Week.

He opened them again to see he was surrounded by girly shit.

Two lady razors—one pink, one purple—hung from plastic holders suction-cupped to the wall. The razors matched the two big mesh poofs of the same colors hanging from the hot and cold water knobs.

Then there was the tiny shelf over crowded with bottles. Raspberry-scented shower gel. Foo-foo brand shampoo and matching conditioner. Then another conditioner, because apparently one wasn't enough.

He didn't care. For the first time in eight weeks he wasn't covered in sand. Wasn't being yelled at. Wasn't cold. Wasn't tired.

Well, maybe he was still a little tired. The fourteen hours he'd slept immediately after the instructors called the end of Hell Week hadn't made up for all he'd missed over those five and a half days.

He'd survived the first phase, when many hadn't. Now he was on a much too short leave before he had to be back for the start of the second phase of BUD/S—eight weeks of dive training.

Not that he was complaining. He loved Coronado.

He'd finish the SEAL training or die trying. But for today he was very happy to be anywhere but there. Maybe that was one reason why he'd hopped in the truck and high tailed it off base without even bothering to shower.

He'd already stopped by for a quick visit with the parents. Then he'd driven directly to see his little sister at college. He'd been ignoring her too much lately.

When he'd arrived at Amanda's dorm and found the note on the suite's door saying she wouldn't be back from class for another half an hour, he realized how rank he smelled. Not surprising after his two and a half hour drive to San Bernardino in the heat in an old truck with a broken A/C.

As long as he had the time, he'd jumped into her shower.

The sound of the bathroom door opening reminded him he must have been in there for a long time if Amanda was back from class.

He wasn't going to worry about the intrusion on his privacy. They'd been forced to share a bathroom growing up so it wasn't the first time she'd busted into the bathroom for something or another while he was in the shower.

Luckily back then, like now, he was behind an opaque curtain. Though it had been a source of many a screaming fight growing up that she so easily invaded his space.

Her irritating habit had made for a few awkward times back in his teen years. Luckily that wasn't the case today. He was too tired even for *that* small pleasure.

He was about to call to her that he'd be right out and hope she'd take the hint and leave when a female voice said, "Oh, my God. Amanda, you're not going to believe what I just heard."

His eyes widened. The person on the other side of the shower curtain obviously wasn't his sister Amanda.

Her roommate. That had to be it. He'd forgotten about her. And he couldn't have known that his sister's bad habit of ignoring a closed door would extend to her college roomie as well.

Shit.

He was going to have to tell her it was him in there, not Amanda, but the girl barely took a breath before she kept going with this apparently incredible news she couldn't wait until her roommate was out of the shower to reveal.

"Delta Sig got a keg and snuck it up in the elevator. It's in their suite right now. I saw it with my own eyes. Tonight we are going to par-tay."

His brows rose. His sister wasn't old enough to drink and even if these Deltas were of age, he doubted a keg was allowed in the dorms on campus.

If—make that *when*—that party got broken up, his sister could get caught in the fray. Possibly expelled.

Or just as bad and equally likely, everyone would be shit-faced. He'd be lucky if Amanda walked away from the night with just a hangover and not something worse—like a sexual assault charge against some drunken college boy.

His fits clenched as tightly as his jaw as his mind spun. He came up with no good scenario that could come of this night.

"Oh, and I'm calling dibs on the room tonight. You'll probably hook up with Jasper anyway so you can go to his room. Summer break is coming so you'd better lock that boy down into a relationship now, if you're smart."

His eyes widened. Who the fuck was Jasper? Whoever he was, there would be no hooking up or locking down tonight.

"And hurry up in the shower so I can get in there. I have to shave my legs because I saw the hottest guy I've ever laid eyes on walking into our dorm like half an hour ago. I can only hope he's here visiting Delta Sig for the party. And if he is—man oh man, he'd better watch out because your girl here is on the prowl tonight. Wait until you see him. Tall. Light brown hair. These gorgeous green eyes. Muscles that barely fit inside his US NAVY T-shirt."

Shit. She was describing him.

The last freaking thing he needed right now was a teenage stalker. He pushed that horror aside. He had more important things to deal with. Like saving his sister from this boy crazy girl on the prowl.

Boys. Booze. This chick was obviously a bad influence. His mind was made up, he was going to just tell Amanda she needed a new roommate. And if she refused, he'd tell their parents what was going on and they'd make her move out of the suite.

In the meantime, he'd have to reveal himself and set this girl straight. And let her know what he thought about her plans for this evening and inform her they would not include his sister.

The sound of the bathroom door opening again halted Zach's hand as he reached for the faucet.

"Gabby, who are you talking to in here?" Amanda asked. "And have you seen my brother? He was supposed to be here by now. I left the door unlocked for him."

Zach twisted the knobs to turn off the water and heard a gasp before Gabby said, "Uh, oh."

After wiping the water out of his eyes, he whipped the top part of the curtain open while holding the bottom part closed. He was just in time to see the wide-eyed panic in Gabby's eyes as she was faced with the evidence of her mistake.

Amanda grinned, obviously realizing what had happened and enjoying it too much.

"Zach, my brother. Gabby, my roommate." She extended her hand to indicate each one of them in turn by way of introduction. "Though it seems you two have already met."

"Not officially. No," he said, taking in the girl he'd heard so much from without being able to see her.

Brown eyes, still widened with horror, were framed with thick lashes. Her dark shiny hair hung straight and long, easily reaching to her hips. And even the deep tone of her skin couldn't hide the red spots in her cheeks.

His mind served up a memory. Amanda all excited after she'd first moved into the dorm for the start of freshman year. She'd told him her roommate was from Hawaii and how cool she thought that was.

This girl was a little too cool for his taste and she'd been a bad influence on his sister for the entire school year. Too long.

He shot her a glare, realizing while he'd been busy

serving the country in the Navy, and more recently with SEAL training, he'd dropped the ball when it came to keeping an eye on his sister and who she was living with.

Gabby met his gaze, then yanked her eyes away. She had been real chatty a moment ago, but apparently now, face-to-face, she'd run out of things to say.

So why were they still standing there in the bathroom?

He cocked up one brow. "Would you both mind leaving so I can get out and get dressed?"

"Sure thing, bro." Still looking annoyingly amused, Amanda turned and left.

Her roommate backed out of the room, bumping into the sink before reaching the doorway. "Nice, um, to meet you," she said, before fleeing and slamming the door behind her.

Zach shook his head, almost afraid to leave the shelter of the curtained stall lest the crazy roommate came back in to say something else.

He finally did and as he toweled off, he added one more thing to his To Do list for today—lecture Amanda about underage drinking and safe sex. Safe sex being, in his opinion and as far as his sister was concerned, *no* sex at all.

This was supposed to be just a quick visit, a couple of hours, maybe including lunch with her, before he left for the two hour drive to La Mesa to have dinner with their grandmother.

He'd prefer to stay here and chaperone that party. Or even better, shut it down altogether. But he'd promised he'd visit their grandmother and she was expecting him tonight.

Once he graduated in a few months, he'd be assigned to a team and precious time with family would become even scarcer. And his grandmother wasn't getting any younger. Who knew how long he'd have her in his life?

Besides, he'd promised her, and he kept his promises, no matter what. He could only hope he'd get a promise out of Amanda to be good tonight—and that she'd keep that promise in spite of her roommate.

He got himself toweled off and dressed, all without further interruption, thank God. But there was nothing to be thankful about when he opened the bathroom door and saw what his sister was wearing.

"What the fuck is that?"

She turned to look at him. "What the fuck is what? And Mom would swat you with the wooden spoon for that word if she heard it."

He was just months away from getting his trident and being a full fledged Navy SEAL, pledging himself body and soul to the teams and the defense of this country, but Amanda was right. His mother would still swat him. The woman recognized no authority except her own.

"Yeah, well, she's not here to hear me. And you know damn well she wouldn't approve of what you're wearing." His gaze hit on her short shorts.

Amanda planted one hand on her hip. "It's a theme party. We have to dress like this."

"What the fuck kind of theme requires that?" Zach scowled at her outfit.

"The Dukes of Hazard," she returned.

"Daisy Duke wears shorts like this," Gabby explained, not so helpfully, as if any man alive didn't know Daisy Duke.

For the first time since entering the room he turned his attention to her—and saw what she was doing.

The girl had a pair of scissors in one hand and a pair of jeans in the other. She was in the midst of hacking off one leg.

"Did you do this?" Zach tipped a chin toward Amanda's nearly obscene shorts. "Made those shorts for her?"

"Um . . ." Gabby's eyes went wide as her lips remained pressed tightly shut.

Zach figured he had his answer.

Amanda took a step forward, as if blocking her friend from him. "Yes, she did. And if she didn't I would have, but she's much better at crafts and stuff than I am."

Zach drew in a breath. "So you're both going to go to this frat party tonight with your asses hanging out? A party where there's going to be an illegal keg?"

"Yes, we are." Amanda folded her arms over her chest and looked fierce. At least as fierce as a teenaged college girl could look.

"Fine." With a sigh, Zach pulled out his cell. Short of tying her up and locking her in the room, there was only one thing to do.

Jaw clenched, he scrolled through the contacts for his grandmother's number. He was going to have to break his promise to the sweetest woman in the world.

She'd probably been cooking all day in preparation for his arrival, all for nothing.

Thanks to little Miss Gabby and her scissors, both his and his grandmother's evenings were about to be ruined. He'd cancel dinner, but he'd never forget why or forgive the girl who'd made him do it.

Sending a glare in Gabby's direction, he made the call and waited for his grandmother to answer.

When she did, he said, "Hi, Grams. I'm so sorry about this but it looks like I'm going to be staying in San Bernardino with Amanda tonight. Can we reschedule dinner?"

CHAPTER TWO

"So, here it is. What do you think?" Gabby gnawed on her lip and waited.

She'd poured her heart and soul into redecorating this room for her best friend.

If she couldn't get it right for Amanda, the woman she'd known and loved for well over a decade, since they'd been freshman in college, then she would know for sure she couldn't do this. Couldn't make a living in the interior design business.

Then what would she do with her life?

"I love it." Amanda interrupted her gloomy thoughts.

Gabby's gaze whipped to her friend. "Do you really?"

"Yes, really. It's amazing. But there's no way you did this on a hundred dollar budget." Amanda lifted a brow. "Tell me what you actually spent and I'll reimburse you."

"No, really. I did it on budget. I swear." Gabby's heart was racing at her friend's approval.

Amanda crossed her arms. "I don't believe you."

She laughed, giddy. High on her success.

Her idea for a redecorating on a budget blog, to be turned into a future book, and maybe even a television show—yeah right, in her dreams—might just work. She might not starve after all while trying to earn a living as a decorator.

"I can prove it to you. I have all the receipts for what I spent on the room." She moved toward the small wooden half-moon table. "I found this at a thrift shop for fifteen dollars. I sanded it down and painted it white and *viola*! It's perfect in your office next to the chair, which was one of the extra armchairs from your dining set, by the way."

She moved to the bookcase.

"The books were on sale at the library for a dollar each. For hardcovers! Can you believe it? Anyway I took off the dust jackets, spun them so the pages are forward and the spines hidden and they really make a statement. And the knickknacks on the shelves were all yours."

"Really?" Amanda frowned, taking a step closer.

"Yup." Gabby nodded. "I found some in your glass front cabinet in the dining room. And a few others were still packed away in boxes in your attic."

Amanda shook her head. "I'll be darned. You're right. I remember getting some of these things as wedding and shower gifts and thinking I'd never use them. But they look great in here."

"Because I chose a color scheme and stuck to it. If you batch different things of similar colors together they make a statement."

Her friend smiled. "And that's why you're the interior designer and I'm a CPA."

Gabby let out a laugh. "Also why you own a great

house and have a steady income and I'm about to be evicted from my apartment."

Amanda frowned. "I hope you're joking."

Gabby lifted a shoulder and her friend's eyes widened.

"Gabby! Tell me. What's going on?"

"My building was sold. The new owners are going to double my rent when my lease is up next month."

Amanda drew in a breath. "Bastards."

"Yup." Gabby nodded, even though name calling wouldn't help her situation.

"Do you need a loan? A place to stay? The guest room is yours if you need it."

"Thank you. I appreciate it. I do, but I'm not moving in with you and Jasper."

Amanda dismissed the concern with the flick of her wrist. "Why not? We've been together seriously since the summer before sophomore year in college and married for five years now. It's not like we're still in the honeymoon period."

Struggling so badly at her chosen career that she needed to take charity from friends was a tough pill to swallow. Six months ago she'd left her job as a sales girl to pursue decorating full time but it looked as if she might be going back.

Gabby shook her head. "What I really want is a design client."

"You'll get one. And until you do, stay here. Please. I'd love to have the company. Jasper works such long hours. It'll be fun. Come on."

"Thank you, but I'm fine. I still have my apartment for now. But I really do need to land one or two big decorating jobs. The money from those, combined with what I have left in my savings, and I'll be able to afford the security deposit and first month's rent on a nice new apartment."

Amanda's eyes narrowed. "Hmm."

"Uh, oh. I know that expression." Gabby had seen it too many times in college. Amanda was a mastermind when it came to plans and schemes.

"I've got one job for you, for sure. A whole house makeover. And I've got a possible client for you for a second job. A retail space."

"Really?" How had Amanda never mentioned all this before? Was she making it all up just to help out? Suspicious, Gabby asked, "What are these jobs?"

"Well, one of my clients is opening a coffee shop type of place. She just bought the building and is starting to tear out the old linoleum floors and florescent fixtures and stuff. I could give her a call. Maybe offer a free consultation with you? You can dazzle her with all your great ideas for décor for the shop and I bet she'll hire you to take over. This is a passion project for her. She's already got her hands full with kids and working part-time for her husband's business."

"Oh my God. That sounds perfect. You'd really call her for me?"

"Of course, I will. I'm getting the number now." Amanda moved toward the desk.

"What's the second job? Who's that client?" Gabby asked.

Amanda paused, cell phone in one hand. "Um, well, that would be me."

Gabby shook her head. "No. I'm not taking your money or redoing this house. It's beautiful. Perfect. I only agreed to do your office because, well, it was hideous before, no offense. And I knew I could do it on the cheap and it made for great content for my blog. And if you did it alone you just would have ordered everything off the IKEA website and I refuse to let my best friend have a boring cookie cutter office. But I'm not doing the whole house for you just because you feel bad for me."

"You're not doing my house. You're going to do my grandmother's house."

Gabby paused. She'd attended Amanda's grandmother's funeral. "Did you inherit her house?"

"Kind of."

"Kind of? What does that mean?"

"Well, Zach and I inherited the estate. And since I already have a house, he took the house and I took the stocks and money. I put it away in a high yield account and swore I would do something with it that would make my grandmother proud. I think this is it."

Gabby shook her head. "There are too many things wrong with this plan for me to even start."

Amanda folded her arms. "What's wrong with it?"

"Well, first off, your brother hates me." He had since the great shower incident at the end of freshman year.

"He doesn't hate you. He just doesn't know you."

Because Gabby had made it a point to stay out of his way. It had been surprisingly easy to avoid seeing him since he was in the Navy and away like all the time.

He'd missed Amanda's wedding and their grandmother's funeral. What kind of man did that?

Amanda said she understood. That as a SEAL Zach had to go where he was told and when, no matter what.

Gabby wasn't so sure she'd be as forgiving if she had a brother and he did that to her. Maybe she just didn't get the sibling thing, being an only child.

Still, her parents were an ocean away in Hawaii and she managed to get there for their thirtieth anniversary party.

That plane ticket had put quite a dent in her small but precious savings account, but that's what family did for family.

The fact remained, she and Zach had gotten off on the wrong foot all those years ago and, judging by the glare and cold welcome he'd delivered the few times she'd seen him since, they still hadn't gotten on the right foot.

She couldn't imagine he'd want her involved in anything having to do with his house.

Gabby leveled a stare on Amanda. "We'll have to agree to disagree. But besides Zach's feelings about me, I refuse to take your inheritance, so forget about it. I'll take the meeting with your client, and thank you for that, but that's it."

Amanda's steady headshaking told Gabby she was in for a battle. "Nope. I've decided. Zach has been living in Grandma's house for two years now and hasn't changed a thing. Except for the weight set in the middle of the living room, the house still looks like an eighty-year old woman lives there. Crocheted doilies and all. It's ridiculous. He'll never get married if that's the house he brings his dates back to."

"He's not dating?" Gabby asked before she could stop herself.

Amanda's brow shot high. Her lips twitched. "No, he's not dating."

Crap. Amanda was too sharp.

Gabby backpedaled. "It's just that at his age, I'd thought he'd be with someone for years already now."

"Nope. He's not. He's still single and available. But seriously, Gabby. Take the job. You'd be doing me and him a favor because I've decided, I'm redoing that house with or without your help."

Gabby drew in a breath. She knew her friend. Amanda would do it on her own. And she'd spend a fortune for cookie cutter, chain store furniture made out of pressboard.

The designer half of Gabby couldn't let that happen any more than the friend half of her could. "Fine. I'll do it."

"Yay! Thank you." Amanda was all smiles. Gabby, on the other hand, was all dread.

She shook her head. "Don't get so excited. I'm telling you, Zach is going to put a stop to this before it even starts. I'm sure of it."

Amanda was still looking too happy about the horrifying prospect of Gabby decorating the home of the man who hated her.

"Nope. He won't because he won't know," she said.

Gabby widened her eyes. "How will he not know?"

Men might be oblivious sometimes, but Gabby thought Zach would notice when things started disappearing and new things appeared in their place, even if she could manage to sneak in the stuff when he wasn't home.

"He's away. He doesn't tell me much, and half of that is probably lies because there is no way he is away at all those 'trainings' with his team." Amanda used air quotes and scowled. "But I know this . . .

16

before he left he said the whole team was deploying for at least a few months and he probably wouldn't be home for my birthday. He gave me my gift early and everything."

"Your birthday isn't until next month." Gabby's pulse picked up speed.

"Right." Amanda smiled. "Can you get his whole place redone before my birthday?"

Her mind spun with plans, ideas and the beginnings of a To Do list. She glanced up and saw Amanda waiting for her answer.

A whole month to redo one small two-bedroom house? And Zach would be out of the country the whole time?

Gabby raised her gaze to her friend. "I'll need a key to get inside."

Amanda smiled. "No problem. I'll give you my copy."

"All right. Then, yeah, I'll get it done." Gabby couldn't control her grin.

CHAPTER THREE

Djibouti was hot as hell. Literally.

Zach could only imagine that the average mean temperature on the Horn of Africa and that of the fires of Hell had to be pretty close.

At least it felt that way as he ran, in full kit, for the aircraft.

Sweat dripped into his eyes. Eyes he couldn't wipe often enough to keep his vision clear.

Inside the Osprey, Zach cursed the heat. "Fuck it. I'm taking this shit off."

Ripping open the fasteners on his vest, he maneuvered across the narrow space and started to throw off equipment, dropping it onto an empty seat.

"What the fuck are you doing, Z-man?" Frowning, Levi *Dutch* Van Der Hayden watched from where he'd already strapped himself in—like Zach should be doing.

"Looks like he's stripping to me. And here I am with no dollar bills." Grinning, Justus Kirkland delivered Zach a wink before he dumped himself into one of the seats. The man folded his bare tattoo-covered arms as if settling in for the show. "Sorry, Z-man. No tip for you today. I'll catch you later."

Zach noticed Justus was wearing the bare minimum he could get away with and still operate. A short-sleeved T-shirt beneath his vest, which was visibly lacking in ballistic plates.

Smart man. Zach was about to join him and lighten his own load. This heat was ridiculous.

Djibouti was hot as fuck normally. He knew this. The team had been here for months. But this afternoon the weather had turned molten.

How could the nighttime temperature be hotter than the day? It made no sense, and neither did the damn shirt he was wearing.

Zach pulled off his new long-sleeved tactical shirt and tossed it. The sweat-soaked fabric hit the floor with a splat. Fuck the shirt and its supposed cooling technology.

Moisture wicking fabric, his ass! If the damn thing didn't make him drip in sweat it wouldn't have to wick it away.

He reached for his vest and slid it on over his bare arms and damp tank top. The thin tank he could deal with.

Immensely happier, he slid into the seat and looked up to see his two teammates still watching him. "What? I was hot."

Cocking up a blonde brow, Dutch scowled. "And I'm not?"

Justus glanced sideways at Dutch before shooting Zach a glance. "Don't listen to Sir Complains-A-Lot over there. I heard bare arms were all the rage this year for the most fashionable special operators."

The joke was ridiculous but still made Zach snort

out a laugh even as he shook his head.

The rest of the guys filed in, one by one. Rio *Compass* North, one of the biggest guys on the team but with a huge heart to match. Tony *Nitro* Gallo, by far the most competitive among them and also the team medic. Vegas boy Aidan *Rocket* Stone was followed by Louisiana-born Thibaut *T-Bone* Cyr.

Finally Jace *Hawk* Hawkins brought up the rear. He took the seat next to Zach but not before dropping his gaze up and down Zach's bare arms.

Preemptively, Zach answered the unasked question. "It's hot."

Hawk dipped his head. "True that. I'll be glad to be back in Montana."

That statement called attention to the elephant in the room—or in the Osprey, as the case may be.

If plans didn't change, the team would be leaving Djibouti in about a week—hopefully less.

Only part of the team would be going back to Coronado to await the next assignment or deployment. Two of them—Hawk and Compass— would be going back to pack up their shit for the final time and head for home to tackle life as a civilian.

The team was about to change. Zach didn't like change.

He wondered whether to address the fact this could very likely be the last mission that SEAL Team Three would be on together. Ever.

Maybe he should leave the subject alone and pretend this was just another op. But Hawk had brought it up. He had been the one to mention going home . . . and not to the team's home on Coronado either.

Zach glanced sideways at his teammate. "You

feeling okay about getting out? You don't think you'll miss it? The rush."

"What are you saying, Z-man? You don't think the family ranch is exciting?" Hawk grinned and then sobered. He drew in a breath and let it out, his gaze meeting and holding Zach's. He lifted one shoulder. "I honestly don't know how I'll feel."

And that raw and honest answer was the same one Zach had given to himself whenever the notion of getting out struck him. It was a lot to think about.

But nobody was getting out today and they had a job to do.

They reached their destination in no time. The Saudi-Yemen border wasn't all that far from Camp Lemonnier and the Osprey was a fast bird.

In under an hour the Marine Corps flight crew had set the aircraft down.

Night vision goggles turned Zach's world green as he led his team out of the aircraft and into the dark night.

"TOC, this is Bravo One. Bravo team has boots on the ground," Zach said into his communicator for the benefit of command back at the tactical operations center.

"Good copy, Bravo One. Now bring me back what you went there for."

If only locating and rescuing the Green Beret taken by the Iranian-backed Houthi rebels were as easy as his lieutenant commander made it sound.

Zach kept his opinions to himself and said, "Copy that."

Intel suggested the rebels had him somewhere in the mountains between Saudi Arabia and Yemen. The Green Berets had been working in the tumultuous border region helping the Saudis take out suspected Houthi missile sites.

A small Special Forces unit had crossed into Yemen. Only eleven of the twelve made it back out. Now, SEAL Team Three's priority was to get that one out . . . preferably alive.

They had a hike ahead of them and time was of the essence. The Osprey had dropped them off on the Saudi side of the border. They'd have to patrol into Houthi territory following a mountain path where satellite imagery had seen a group of men traveling with what looked liked a hostage.

His team's mission was to scope out the situation. Determine if the hostage was the Green Beret. Take him, by stealth or force, depending on what they found, then get the hell out of there.

And ideally they had to do it all before sunrise.

Sure. No problem. Piece of cake.

Zach fought the urge to roll his eyes and turned to his team. "All right. Let's move out. We've got a long way to go."

"The fun never ends," Justus hiked the strap of his weapon higher.

"I hate patrolling. Give me a HALO jump any day over this shit." Dutch grumbled as the group took off.

Next to Zach, Hawk let out a short laugh. "I can tell you one thing I'm not gonna miss. I'm not gonna miss listening to Dutch's bitching."

Zach smiled at the truth of that, but that was the end of his good humor. A soldier's life was in their hands. There was no time to waste.

They moved out, slowly traversing the distance from the drop zone to the path. There they picked up the pace, moving swift and sure along the darkened roadway.

"Bravo One, we've got you on thermal. Target is approximately one klick, dead ahead." The communication from command told Zach they'd made good time.

In an hour, the team had caught up to the group ahead of them.

A small group of trained men in top physical condition traveling light—or as light as they could while still being armed and ready for anything—could move much faster than the larger group of locals transporting a hostage.

Zach held up one bent arm. Behind him, the team halted. "Copy that, TOC. How many combatants?"

"Twenty-four fighters plus what appears to be one captive."

"Is the captive mobile?" Zach asked.

"He's on his feet. Looks like he's bound by the hands and being led with a rope," the lieutenant commander replied.

That he was walking was good news. It would slow the team down if they had to carry this guy out.

"Where is he positioned within the group?" Zach asked.

"Dead center."

That figured.

It would be too much to ask for the guy they were there to retrieve to be walking in the back of the pack where they could pluck him away from the group and disappear into the darkness.

"Copy. Going quiet until we've got him."

"Good copy," the lieutenant replied. "Talk to you on the other side."

Zach turned to his team. "It doesn't look like we can do this the easy way."

Compass blew out a breath. "'Course not."

"When we're right on top of them we'll take out the back half of the group. Choose and call your targets. On my signal, we drop the first eight all at once. That should cause enough confusion to scatter the rest of them. Do not lose sight of that soldier. Hopefully he'll get forgotten in the scuffle, but I'm not going to plan on that. And for God's sake, don't accidentally shoot him."

Rocket let out a snort at that order.

Zach ignored him and signaled them forward. Time to get their man.

CHAPTER FOUR

"What's on today's agenda for project Surprise Big Brother?" Amanda asked.

Gabby rolled her eyes at Amanda's code name for the decorating job. "Let's hope it's not more like project Strangle the Designer. And today's To Do list is paint all the trim here and order the tile for your client's coffee shop."

She cradled the cell phone on one shoulder as she tried to pry open a can of paint with a screwdriver.

Maybe she'd splurge on a blue tooth earpiece for herself after she got paid for these two jobs. She'd gotten so used to pinching every penny after college as she tried to make a go of it here in California on her own—without help from her parents—she hadn't allowed herself anything optional.

Now, with not one but two jobs, and one of them pretty huge, she might be willing to ease up on her tight budget. Maybe.

The cell slipped and she caught it just before it fell into the gallon of white semi-gloss trim paint.

Okay, maybe an earpiece was less of a splurge and

more of a safety measure.

She hit the screen to put the call on speakerphone and set it down on the floor before she grabbed the narrow angled brush.

"Ooo, that sounds exciting," Amanda cooed.

"Which part?"

"Both. I want to come with you to order the tile. Can I?"

"No. And I noticed you didn't say you want to come over and help me paint your brother's baseboards and window trim."

"Yeah, no. You don't want me painting anyway. I suck at it. Jasper won't let me touch a paint brush anymore after the great gallon spillage of twenty-fourteen."

Gabby cringed. "I don't blame him."

"But that's still no reason to not let me come with you to the tile store. You're just being mean."

Gabby could picture her friend's face. Even Amanda's words sounded pouty.

"I'm not being mean. She already picked the tile. Today I'm just placing the order over the phone."

"Bummer. Oh well. I'll just have to see it when it's installed."

"Good plan," Gabby agreed.

Some people had two left feet. Her best friend had two left everything. It would be safer for everyone if she just came to admire the work after both places were done.

And speaking of being done . . . "So after this, all the big renovation stuff is done for Zach's place. Then all I have to do is start on the furnishings."

"Wow. That's great."

"It is, but I'm still on a tight timeline. Have you

heard from him about when exactly he'll be home?" Gabby asked.

Amanda let out a snort. "I can tell you have no experience with the military. SEALs in particular. There's no *exactly* anything. And even if he could estimate when he'd be back, he wouldn't tell me. Between transportation delays and operational security, the best I get is an estimate."

"And the latest estimate is?" Gabby prompted.

"He said hopefully he'd be home around my birthday."

"That's a pretty wide window of time. What if he comes home tomorrow instead of next month?" Wet paintbrush in one hand, Gabby stopped before dipping it into the can again.

"I have faith in you. You can get it done. And if experience has taught me anything, Zach is usually home later rather than sooner. You'll be fine."

She wasn't as sure as her friend.

Gabby sighed. "Okay, let me get back to work, just in case you're wrong."

"Worry wart. Call me later. I want to come with you if you go furniture shopping."

Gabby paused. She was planning on less shopping and more dumpster diving. She had a feeling Amanda wouldn't be up for that. And Zach definitely would not be on board with having furnishings that were once someone else's trash, even if she had scored some of her best finds along the curb on junk day.

Now was not the time to start explaining her upcycling philosophy to her friend, so she agreed, "All right. Will do. Bye."

Gabby disconnected the call and glanced at the clock on her cell's display. The day was flying by. She had no time to waste.

It had taken her almost a month but she'd gotten a ton done. It looked like a different house inside. Gone was the hideously dated avocado green kitchen and pink bathroom tile, replaced with perennial white that would never go out of style.

She'd also spent way too much time up on a ladder scraping off the remains of the old popcorn ceiling.

That had taken forever but it had to be done. Besides the fact it was damaged and falling off in places, she couldn't stand the pebbled surface. So she'd scraped and repainted the ceiling and the walls herself, because dang professional painters were expensive.

But the biggest change in the house came when she'd ripped up the old carpets and discovered the hardwood floors beneath. That had made a huge difference. The whole house seemed fresher, brighter. Like it belonged in this decade.

And now—bonus—Gabby had experience operating the professional sander she'd rented from the local home store. She could only imagine how handy that skill would be for future projects.

All in all—angry big brother and the potential of his killing her with his bare hands aside—this project was going great. Amazing. So much better than she'd expected.

But none of it would matter if Zach got home early and found the project not done. She'd feel like a failure. Worse, he'd see her as one.

She'd long ago given up on any fantasy that her best friend's brother would be interested in her romantically. Now she'd be happy if he just showed her a little bit of respect, or hell, acknowledged her presence with more than a scowl.

This project was her big hope to win him over. She wasn't going to mess it up.

CHAPTER FIVE

The first eight Houthi fell to the unseen enemy hidden by the darkness. That sent the rest running.

They tried to pull their captive with them as they fled, but the soldier couldn't run.

Hell, he was barely walking. He dropped to his knees on the ground and none of the Houthi were willing to drag or carry him. They left him there, abandoning their captive in favor of saving themselves.

"Should we go after them?" Hawk asked, poised on the balls of his feet as the remaining enemy combatants disappeared into the night.

"No. We've got what we came for." Zach moved toward the man on his knees in the road. "Sergeant Thomas Manning?"

The figure nodded. "Yeah."

Zach let out a breath in relief. "Am I glad to see you. Nitro, you're with our guest. Let's get the hell out of here before they regroup and come back."

"Gotcha. Can you walk?" Nitro asked the soldier.

He nodded, accepting Nitro's hand and standing,

and Zach felt another weight lift off his shoulders.

"Good. Here you go." Nitro handed the soldier a pair of NVGs. "Helps to see where we're going."

True that. And as far as he could see, the Houthi were lacking in night vision wear, but this was still their home turf. The enemy had that advantage.

Zach glanced around. They were too exposed. He didn't like it. But to leave the road and try to make their way back over the rocks just to take advantage of the small amount of cover would take too long and leave them exposed for longer.

He turned toward the soldier. The man had been walking for hours and it showed. "How fast can you travel?" Zach asked.

"I wasn't going to rush to my beheading for them, but to get the fuck out of here—I can run."

"Good." Zach didn't come all this way to die on a goat path in fucking Yemen. "We move fast and we might get out of here with no holes in us. Nitro, you and Manning set the pace up in front. I'll watch our sixes. Hawk you're with me."

Nitro set a quick pace, one Zach knew they wouldn't be able to maintain for long. Not with Manning in rough shape.

They'd slow down—later—when they'd put some miles between them and the Houthi. The rebels had lost their prize. Zach had a feeling they weren't going to give up that easily.

The team had to have gone close to five miles at a brisk run when Nitro, who'd been up in front of them, fell back and matched his pace to Zach's. "Manning can't keep up this pace."

He had pushed them all hard. Too hard. Zach wouldn't make Manning run, but he wasn't going to let him sit either. The exfil point, and safety, was too damn close to risk resting.

"All right. Slow it down but we can't stop."

"Understood." Nitro nodded and rejoined Manning, both slowing to a fast walk.

They could all rest once they were safely on the aircraft and headed back to Djibouti.

One more mile, maybe less, and they'd be home free.

"Hug the edge. Let's not make it easy for them to pick us off." Zach veered to the side of the path. It wasn't as smooth there, but it at least afforded them some rock outcroppings and scrubby trees nearby to use as cover if he needed it.

His boot hit a rock on the road and Zach pitched forward just as he felt the whiz of the bullet pass his ear.

"We're taking fire!" He dove off the path and into the bushes. Pitiful cover but it was better than nothing.

He crawled a little farther and made it behind a small tree as the team began to return fire.

They'd moved fast but not fast enough. They'd run out of time. The Houthi were back for their prize, and now they had their hopes of taking eight more US troops as motivation.

Well, they'd touch that soldier or any of his team over Zach's dead body.

"This is Bravo One. We're under attack," Zach radioed in.

"Say again your last, Bravo One."

Zach swung his weapon from behind the cover of his much too small tree trunk and returned fire before repeating, "We are pinned down and taking fire.

Requesting air support."

"Copy. We've got your location as approximately one klick from the exfil point. Close air support two minutes out. Paint your location."

"Copy that."

Hawk hit the ground next to him and sunk low behind a big rock. "So much for getting in and out, quick and quiet."

Pressed against the trunk, Zach said, "Just wanted to make what could be our last op as a team memorable."

"A little less memorable would have been good, thanks." Hawk winced as bullets sent pieces of bark flying over their heads.

"Bravo Five, how's the package?" Zach asked.

He could handle getting shot at, but if they lost the soldier—their entire reason for being here—the whole mission would be for shit.

"Alive," Nitro answered.

Zach had been hoping for a little bit more from the medic, but if he could only have one word, *alive* was a good one.

He didn't have time for chit-chat anyway. True to his promise, the commander would deliver on the close air support.

"Bravo team, lasers, lasers, lasers! Paint your location or go home in a box. The boys in the sky are about to rain down hell all around us. Danger close. Copy?"

He heard a round of verifications from the team as he did what he'd directed them to and used the hand held laser to paint his location so the aircraft would avoid firing on his little sanctuary behind the tree.

As their guardian angels in the sky showered the

surroundings with gunfire, tracer rounds cascaded toward the ground like so many shooting stars.

"Woo hoo! Take that, mother fuckers!" Compass bellowed toward the unseen enemy.

"Z-man! Our ride's here," Rocket's voice came over the communicator.

Beneath the noise of gunfire and the engines of the close air support, Zach had missed the sound of the Osprey's arrival, but Rocket was in a position to see it.

"Copy that. Nitro, get the package on that bird now! Rocket, cover him!"

"Moving out," Nitro said.

"Copy. I've got his six." Rocket confirmed.

Zach glanced at Hawk and asked, "Ready to get the fuck out of Dodge?"

Hawk said, "Thought you'd never ask."

Zach drew in a breath and issued the order, "Bravo team—exfil, exfil, exfil!"

Zach and Hawk leap frogged toward the Osprey set down on the ground a hundred meters from where they'd been pinned. Zach saw Nitro and the soldier disappear inside, followed by Rocket, and felt the relief that one hurdle was down.

Now to get the rest of the team on board and get the fuck off this God-forsaken mountain.

He saw the easily identifiable figures of Compass and T-Bone, the team's two tallest, load on, followed by Justus's wide bulk.

The air support maintained covering fire as he signaled for Hawk to make a run for the bird.

Zach followed and leapt on. He did a quick head count . . . and came up short.

"Where the fuck is Dutch?" he asked, eyes wide.

Fuck. He moved toward the hatch and saw the missing SEAL running full out toward the Osprey.

The sound of bullets pinging against the fuselage had Zach and Hawk, the two closest to the exit ramp, swinging their weapons and peppering the area on either side of Dutch.

Boots pounding, he leapt the last few feet up the cargo ramp and landed with a thud.

"We're all here! Go, go, go!" Zach yelled to the crew while Hawk and Justus laid down a few more hundred rounds before retreating inside as the tilt-rotor aircraft lifted off the ground.

"I'm hit." Dutch's gasped words caught Zach's attention. He turned to see the SEAL clutching at his hip and thigh with both hands.

"Where?" Zach asked.

T-Bone grinned. "In his ass."

"It's not funny, douche face." Dutch shot the man a glare. "I'm lucky I could still run to get to the bird."

"Come on. Admit it. It's a little bit funny." Rocket held his thumb and forefingers together.

"Don't worry, Dutch," Compass said. "You're so little I could've carried you on board." The big man grinned, which only deepened Dutch's scowl.

Nitro left the rescued soldier, strapped in and clutching a water bottle, and made his way toward them with a med bag in his hand. He tipped a chin toward Dutch. "Let me see."

The team cleared a path and Nitro kneeled next to Dutch.

"There's an entry and an exit wound. Looks like it went clean through. In and out. You need to get it taken care of when we get back to camp. Medical is going to want to stitch it up and load you full of antibiotics." Nitro pulled on a pair of blue latex gloves from the med kit. "I can clean it out and patch you up for now. Take off your pants."

Justus chuckled. "I bet that's the first time Dutch has heard *that* in recent memory. From anybody, male or female."

Zach shook his head. "All right. Leave Dutch alone. I gotta call command with a sit rep. I don't need them hearing all your juvenile ass jokes."

Amid a symphony of mixed groans and chuckles from the team, Zach settled himself into a seat.

"*Ow*. Fuck! What the hell are you doing back there?" Dutch whined as he laid face down in the narrow aisle between the inward facing seats as his teammates watched like it was a sporting event.

"Cleaning and butterflying the damn hole in your ass, that's what," Nitro answered. "Stay still."

"Just leave that one hole in the middle between his cheeks open. He needs that one," Justus grinned.

Next to Zach, Hawk shook his head. "Definitely a memorable op."

Zach let out a sigh. "Yup."

And he was definitely looking forward to getting home.

CHAPTER SIX

"How much per square foot?" Gabby paused with the pint of exterior polyurethane in one hand and her ever-present cell phone in the other.

"Fifty-eight dollars," the salesclerk said on the phone.

"A foot?" she asked, not believing her ears. The clerk must have given her the case price or something.

"A square foot. Yes."

"Um, I'll have to get back to you. Thanks for your help." She disconnected the call on the cell and plunked the can down onto the hardware store's counter with a sigh.

The bored looking girl reached for the can and scanned the price. "Anything else?" she asked.

"No, just that." Gabby slipped her credit card onto the counter, mumbling, "Can't buy anything else if I want to afford tile."

She'd promised Amanda's client, now her client, she'd get this job done on budget. To make that happen she was going to have to find hand-painted

Mexican tile somewhere for less, or convince the client to settle for different, cheaper tile.

Darn it. Changing the tile was going to alter the whole ambience of the shop.

"Problems?"

The question came from behind Gabby. Her purchase and receipt in her hand, she turned to see a man behind her. He was wearing kneepads and was covered in dust. But what was really interesting about him was the logo on his T shirt. Manny's Tile & Flooring.

"Yeah. The tile my client likes is fifty-eight dollars a square foot."

"Ouch." He cringed. "What kind is it?"

She opened the picture app on her cell and turned it to face him. "That kind. Hand painted. Mexican."

He frowned at the picture. "Where'd you get that price quote from?"

"San Diego Tile."

"No wonder." He thrust the phone back at her, his disdain for the vendor clear in his narrowed eyes and twisted mouth.

"They'll give me the contractor's price—ten percent off," Gabby said, defending her choice.

Not to mention the client had gone there on her own and decided that out of all the thousands of tiles available, the hand painted Mexican tile was what she needed to have.

Apparently the woman wasn't all that good at math since she didn't realize that fifty-eight dollars a square foot times one thousand square feet equaled fifty-eight thousand dollars and put them way over budget.

He let out a huff. "Hell, that place should give you

a discount considering they probably paid five dollars a foot for that tile themselves."

Gabby understood well the way retail worked. The store had to cover all their cost of doing business, plus make a profit. She didn't begrudge them their mark-up—but she couldn't afford it either.

Which brought her to the real thing she was interested in finding out . . .

"So, where could I go to buy tile like this wholesale?" She had an SUV and a strong back. Why shouldn't she cut out the middleman?

He lifted one shoulder. "There are a bunch of tile places right across the border."

Across the border.

Her heart rate sped. "That close?"

He nodded.

She could drive over and back in a day. After she added a standard industry mark-up to the wholesale price, she'd even make a nice little profit on the trip while still saving the client literally thousands of dollars on the retail price.

"You don't happen to have a name or number of one of these places, do you?"

Her dusty savior pulled out his cell. "Hang on. I'll call the office. The guy I work for probably has all that information on one of the invoices. He's always taking the truck to Tijuana."

"Thank you." Gabby's pulse pounded with anticipation and a little bit with fear. She'd never been to Tijuana, but how bad could it be?

If this worked out, it could be the biggest thing to happen in her business since landing this shop renovation job. To be able to give her clients—when she got more than these two—a better price while making a bigger cut herself would be incredible. Amazing.

It would give her an advantage over the other designers in the area. It could put her over the top. Her mind spun with plans and possibilities.

Maybe she could start sourcing all of her own materials and offer clients unique items that only she could get. Handmade furniture. Pottery. Art and accessories.

She could eventually buy a bigger truck to drive over the border and fill it up with amazing finds. Just imagine what treasures she might discover.

The tile guy leaning on a display shelf and scribbling with a marker on the back of a receipt drew Gabby's attention back to reality.

Finally, he hung up with his boss and thrust the golden ticket to designer stardom toward her. "Here you go. This is the place he buys from."

Hands shaking with excitement, Gabby took the key to her future success. "Thank you. Thank you so much."

"No problem." He glanced at his cell. "I gotta get to a job. Good luck with the tile."

"Thanks." Gabby watched him go and glanced around the store.

With the man gone and the clerk behind the counter still looking uninterested, there wasn't anyone for her to share her joy with.

Gabby had to come up with something to do with all the excitement-fueled energy from scoring such an amazing tip on the tile.

Dumpster diving for fixtures and accessories for Zach's house might be just the thing.

With renewed excitement, she stashed the can of

polyurethane for Zach's front doorsill on the floorboard of her car and started the engine.

She pulled out of the parking spot and heading for the shopping center—the location of the best dumpster diving in Southern California.

One hour later she was pulling up to her apartment with a treasure trove of finds in the back.

A set of brand new but less than perfect shutters she'd squealed when she'd seen leaning against the dumpster behind Home Depot.

The wooden wine box behind the liquor store was the perfect place to hide cords and electronics. With a power strip and a hole drilled in the back it would make a great charging station. With the addition of some sturdy wide fabric ribbon, she was going to create a stand for it out of the wooden snack table legs with the missing top.

Along the curb when she'd turned into her neighborhood, she'd picked up a small wooden table with a single drawer and a nicked blonde wood finish. With light sanding and a fresh coat or two of white paint, it would look great as a nightstand in Zach's bedroom.

She'd even picked up a little something for herself. A set of small ornate gold frames leaning against the building behind the frame shop. They were beautiful in their own right, without any art inside. She loved the quirky idea of empty frames. Those would hang just as they were on the wall of her bedroom.

Why the shop had tossed them, she had no idea. They weren't even really dinged up. And even if they were, she could just paint them.

People were silly.

Tired, but too jazzed to sit still, she figured she'd

grab something to eat at her place, then head over to Zach's tonight to start on the table. She'd rather sand it in his garage than in her two room overstuffed apartment where the dust would settle everywhere on everything.

That was the plan and it was a good one.

Key in hand, she shoved it into the lock, just like she'd done a thousand times before.

When it didn't fit, she looked down at the keychain. She must have tried the wrong key in the lock.

Now that she had Zach's key as well as her own on the ring with her car key, it made sense she'd accidentally grabbed the wrong one.

But no, that one was Zach's and this one should be hers. She turned it the other direction. Still it didn't fit. Then she noticed the lock on the door was shinier than usual. Almost like it was brand new . . .

"No." Her eyes widened as realization hit. "No, no, no, no."

In a panic, she fumbled for her cell and glanced at the date.

It was already the thirtieth. Shit. How the hell had that happened? She had to be out of her apartment by the first of the month. In her mind the first was sometime next week.

She recited the old childhood rhyme to herself. *Thirty days has September, April, June*—crap. April only had thirty days. The first was tomorrow, not next week.

And double crap, the only new apartment complex she'd found that she could afford was terrible.

That was one reason why she'd been dragging her feet about moving. She didn't want to put down a deposit and lock into a lease for someplace crappy.

If she could just wait another couple of weeks, until after she'd gotten paid for these two jobs, she'd have enough money to afford the deposit and first couple of months' rent on a better place.

All of her grand plans for monetary windfalls and nice apartments didn't matter now, because she was locked out. And her stuff was still inside.

Why was she locked out? The notice from the new landlord had said she had until the first. Didn't it?

She scrolled to the building superintendent's number in her contact's list.

"Hello?" he answered.

"Hi, it's Gabrielle Lee. From 1B. I just came home and found the locks changed on my apartment."

"Yup. You had to be out by the first."

"And the first isn't until tomorrow. So to me that means I have until tomorrow to get out."

"And to the new owner it means you should be out today by the close of business so the new renter can move in tomorrow. It's after six p.m.. The locksmith came at five."

Shit. She did not need this right now. "But I didn't move any of my stuff out yet."

"Then I suggest you do that," he said without an ounce of empathy.

"But it's locked." Her voice started to shake as the tears pricked behind her eyes.

He sighed. "I have the key. I can let you in."

Her breath came out in a whoosh of relief. "Thank you so much."

"Yeah, no problem. I also got a truck and a couple of sons, if you need me to help you move your stuff out and to your new place."

There was still compassion and good people in the world.

"Oh my God. That would be so amazing. Thank you."

"Where you moving to?" he asked.

That question whacked down the hope that had fluttered to life and taken flight inside her. There, on the welcome mat whose sentiment mocked her, it rolled over and died a slow stuttering death.

She didn't have an answer to his question. She didn't have a place to move to. She was homeless.

Going home to her parents in Hawaii was not an option right now. How could she finish her work here if she was living there?

She couldn't just show up on Amanda's doorstep tonight with an apartment's worth of stuff and zero notice. She already owed her friend too much for getting her the two jobs.

Thoughts of Amanda and the decorating jobs led to thoughts of Zach and his house. His empty house. With the nearly empty garage.

Maybe she did have someplace to go after all.

Amanda swore he wouldn't be home early. That his return would be closer to her birthday, which was Memorial Day weekend. That gave her a solid three weeks.

It could work. She could stash all her belongings in his garage for now while she looked for a better place.

Hell, she could even sleep there. Who would know? She'd spent so much time in his house painting and refinishing floors, she was almost living there as it was.

And without the time spent fighting traffic driving back and forth to her own place, she'd have extra time every day to work on the decorating jobs so she could get them done even faster.

She could finish both jobs before he got back, get paid and move everything into her new place before he ever got back.

She liked the idea much better than imposing on Amanda and having to admit to her friend that she'd been such a ditz she didn't even know what day it was and had forgotten to move out.

For better or worse, her decision was made. "La Mesa," she finally answered.

"Nice area," the man commented.

"Actually, it's a friend's place where I'll be staying for a few weeks."

Friend. Best friend's brother who hated her. Whatever.

With any luck, no one would ever know.

CHAPTER SEVEN

It was long past dark when Zach turned his truck down the street that would lead to his house . . . or rather, his late grandmother's house.

His grandmother had left it to him and his sister in her will. Since Amanda was a happily married homeowner, they'd split the estate, with Zach taking the house and Amanda the rest.

It wasn't very far from base, and had plenty of room for him and his stuff, but he'd trade it all to have his grandmother back, alive and well while he still lived in the bachelor barracks.

But life hadn't given him that choice so he lived in her house, just the way she'd left it, surrounded by the memories of her and the happy times he'd spent here with her.

It had been a long trip home from Djibouti, but home, sweet home was just a block away. He approached it with mixed emotions.

For months he'd been with the team, twenty-four/seven. To be without them now felt like he'd lost a limb.

To be alone with his own thoughts and the knowledge that he didn't have to listen for a footstep behind him, or the whizz of a bullet or the shrill of a siren, was odd.

Peace at this point was disconcerting. A little chaos would have been welcome. At least it would be familiar.

What wasn't familiar was the car in his driveway. Or actually, it was less car and more SUV, packed to the roof with stuff and parked in front of his house. A house where every light was on.

What the hell?

He slammed on the brakes and cut the lights, letting the truck idle along the curb as he stared at his house, lit up like a damn Christmas tree.

Maybe his post deployment leave wasn't going to be uneventful after all.

He reached for the weapon that had been strapped to him for months and found it missing.

It was back on base, locked up with the rest of his kit. All he had with him was a duffle bag filled with dirty laundry.

He spun to look behind him. He hadn't been in this truck in months. He'd left it parked on base and had one of the guys who was stateside start it up and run the engine every once in a while. But he must have something inside to use as a weapon—

Ah ha! His golf bag was behind him. Perfect. He cut the engine and released the seatbelt.

Twisting in the seat he pulled out a driver and then thought better of it. That club was too lightweight. He slid the driver back in and pulled out the seven iron.

The seven iron was without a doubt the most all

around useful club in the game of golf and, in a pinch, for impromptu home defense.

Armed and ready, he slid the switch on the overhead dome light to *off* so it wouldn't illuminate and then he opened the door, slipping out of the truck and into the darkness.

The thief was either incredibly stupid or insanely brazen. Zach didn't know which but the guy had backed his SUV right up to the garage, like he owned the place.

What Zach did know was that the burglar had already hit another house before his. One glance at the contents of the overstuffed vehicle with the flashlight he always had with him told Zach this wasn't his stuff.

Where the hell did the robber think he was going to fit anything else? Not that Zach had anything in the house to steal anyway. Anything valuable—his equipment, his weapons—were locked up on base. What was left in the house had only sentimental value because it had belonged to his grandmother.

Okay, he had made one major purchase when he'd moved it. A sixty-inch flat screen television. Easily enough replaced, yes, but that wasn't the point. God help the burglar if he'd messed with Zach's favorite new toy.

If he got a hold of the thief, the guy would be getting a taste of the swing that had yielded him a hole-in-one a few years ago at the Sea n' Air Golf Course on the North Island Naval Air Station.

And shit—the ball he'd done it with was in this house too, sitting on the bookcase in front of his grandmother's old books.

The TV and the golf ball. That made two things

the robber—who was about to have a headache when Zach got through with him—had better not have touched.

And crap, the scorecard from that game with the other guys' signatures on it was in there too.

Okay. That made three things—scorecard, ball, TV.

As Zach's mental list of his most valuable worldly possessions slowly expanded, he pressed himself up against the wall of the house, sliding along the foundation as silently as he could while trying to avoid the scrubby shrubs growing there.

Make that the *prickly* scrubby shrubs.

What the hell? Were those thorns on that damn bush? It had never flowered, as far as he knew, so why the fuck was this prickly thing planted here?

As the shrub grabbed onto Zach's cargo shorts and legs, tearing at both the fabric of his clothes and his skin, he cursed himself for not having taken more of an interest in the landscaping.

He certainly would now, once this takedown was over.

In fact, he was on leave. He'd already checked in at base and the next couple of weeks were his own. Gardening hadn't been on the agenda but he could squeeze in taking a machete to this damn killer plant.

A woman's voice halted both his thoughts and his movement. From his place outside the open bathroom window he heard clearly the sound of the water running in the shower and a woman singing.

He knew the window had been closed and locked when he'd left for Djibouti months ago. It should still be locked unless Amanda had been by and opened the windows for some reason—

Amanda.

Was it his sister who'd parked in his driveway and was singing in his bathroom? And what the hell was that she was singing, anyway?

Was that a Disney song? It sure had that unmistakable sound to it.

Zach had a sudden recollection from his childhood of Amanda seated in front of the television with a DVD in the player, singing along at the top of her lungs to some animated film.

Yup, it had to be Amanda inside.

Her singing sounded a lot better today than it had back then, when she'd bellowed along, dressed in a pastel frilly dress and pretending she was the princess on screen.

With a sigh, he relaxed, falling out of SEAL mode and into annoyed brother mode instead.

Why was she here and showering at his house, and with a strange vehicle filled with a butt load of stuff?

Shit. Had something bad happened between her and her husband? He liked Jasper. He'd hate to have to kill his brother-in-law for hurting his sister.

Loosening his grip on the club, he reached into his pocket and drew out his house key. Opening the front door, he stepped inside.

Intruder-scare aside, it felt good to be home in the land of free flowing Big Macs and reliable WiFi. Not to mention private bathrooms—which he was going to have again as soon as he determined why the fuck his sister was in his and got her out of it.

Zach leaned the golf club in the corner of the front hallway and looked around. Why did it smell like paint? That question was soon answered when he noticed the walls.

Why the fuck was the hallway a different color? And where was the carpet? He frowned down at the shiny wooden floors before his gaze moved on to the living room.

Where was the furniture? And where the fuck was his TV?

He might actually have felt better thinking he had been robbed. At least that was something he could get angry about. But this—this was worse because he had a strong suspicion about what was really going on here.

Amanda must have suggested a dozen times that he redecorate. He'd always said no. Then he'd deployed, leaving his nosy, annoying, untrustworthy sister alone for months with his spare house key.

Jaw clenched, he stomped across the gleaming wood of the empty living room and down the hallway. He resisted the urge to kick in the bathroom door and instead flung it wide with a force that sent it crashing against the wall.

"What the fuck did you do to my house?"

The blood curdling scream that came from behind the new shower curtain gave him a moderate sense of satisfaction.

Good. He was glad he'd startled her, because she sure as hell had surprised him.

"I swear, Amanda. I told you I liked my house just the way it was—"

"Zach. It's not Amanda." The tiny voice from behind the curtain halted his rant.

Brows drawn low, he reached for his cell phone to call the police.

Not that he thought he couldn't take whoever was in that shower stall, but more because he wanted witnesses for his own sake. A woman who would break into a man's house to take a shower might not stop there. What was to stop her from claiming Zach attacked her?

But wait. She'd called him by name, so he obviously knew her. Or at least, she knew him. With the screen unlocked and his fingers poised to dial nine-one-one, Zach said, "Who are you?"

"It's Gabby."

He was wondering who the fuck this Gabby could be, racking his brain for some memory of a long forgotten hook-up who could have gotten a hold of a copy of his house key, when she pulled back just the top of the curtain, while clutching the bottom closed.

She zeroed in on his frown and continued, "Amanda's friend. From college."

The dark hair. The big brown eyes. The *oh shit* expression on her face. It all brought the memory of the first time he'd set eyes on her back to him.

They'd played out this scene together before, only last time he'd been on the other side of that curtain.

"What are you doing in my house?" He lowered the cell phone, but didn't put it away.

His next call was going to be to his sister to tell her to get the hell down here and get her insane friend out of his shower.

He'd only seen this girl—now a woman—a handful of times since that first meeting.

Somehow Amanda hadn't outgrown her college friend and Gabby, like a bad penny, kept turning up at occasional major events in Amanda's life that they both attended. He usually managed to stay out of her way, and she out of his.

He'd get through the party or family barbecue or

whatever it was by ignoring her. He couldn't ignore her now. And he was still waiting for an answer.

"Could you turn off the damn water? We're in the middle of a drought." He scowled.

She disappeared and did as told, then was back, but she still wasn't explaining her presence fast enough for his liking.

"Amanda hired me to redecorate your place. As a surprise for you. I'm a designer now. Gabrielle Lee Interiors and More." She paused, as if waiting for him to say something. When he didn't, she continued, "You weren't supposed to be home until next month. I'm not done yet."

Oh, so now it was his fault for coming home early.

He crossed his arms over his chest. "That doesn't explain why you're in my shower."

"Yeah, I know."

Zach leaned back against the doorframe. He could wait as long as is took but he wasn't leaving until he had a proper explanation.

"I lost my apartment and I haven't found a new one yet. It was only going to be for a few weeks."

His eyes widened. "Are you kidding me? You were just going to squat in my house until I got back?"

"It wasn't going to be exactly squatting. I was going to work here, day and night, to get everything done in time."

"And sleep here. And shower here," he added.

"Well, yeah." She finally raised her eyes to meet his. "I'm sorry. I just wanted it to be nice when you got home."

"Oh, I see. You're doing it for me." He shook his head. "You were bad news then and you're still bad news now. I warned Amanda about you. She

53

obviously didn't listen."

A spark of anger flamed to life in her eyes. "I am not. You never gave me a fair chance. Never tried to get to know me. You should know Amanda wouldn't be my best friend if I were as horrible of a person as you think I am. And I don't even know why you hate me so much. Just because I walked in on you in the shower when I thought it was Amanda? So what? Boo hoo, big bad SEAL had his privacy invaded. What were you doing in *my* shower that day anyway? Huh?"

Something about her trying to look intimidating while clutching a shower curtain had him smiling, and then outright laughing.

This kind of shit only happened to him. The guys weren't going to believe it when he told them. It was too crazy.

"Oh, man." He ran a hand over his face, controlling himself enough to speak. "Look, I've been traveling for three days. I'm tired, hungry and a little punchy. I want a cold beer, some hot wings and then I wanna sleep in my own bed."

He had a bad feeling his bed might no longer be here, but he'd deal with that later, after the naked crazy chick was out of his house.

"I'm going out," he continued. "I expect you to be gone when I get back."

She bit her lip and didn't answer.

"What now?" he asked, afraid of the reply.

"All of the stuff from my apartment is in your garage. I can sleep at Amanda's tonight, but I can't get everything out until tomorrow."

He looked skyward, seeking patience. "Fine."

"Zach."

He'd already turned to go when her voice stopped him.

"Yeah?" He planted his hand on the doorframe but didn't look back, waiting for whatever she had to say.

"Don't be mad at Amanda. She just wanted to do something nice for you."

"I didn't ask her to," he reminded.

"I know. I told her it was a bad idea."

Now he did turn to look at her. "Did you?"

"Yes." Gabby tipped her head in a nod. "But she insisted."

Score one for the crazy chick. Even she knew redoing a man's home while he was away was a hugely bad idea. Too bad Amanda didn't listen.

"Will you let me at least finish the house?" she asked.

That was the last thing he wanted.

His knee jerk reaction was to put everything back the way it had been before his sister and her crazy college roommate had meddled with it. But he had a feeling that ship had passed.

Likely his grandmother's old carpet was in a landfill somewhere. He'd see the old wallpaper he'd grown up with had been painted over or stripped.

He evaluated the situation and decided the absolute last thing he wanted was to have to finish redecorating his damn house during his leave. But he at least wanted to have some say in finishing it. It was his house.

Gabby and Amanda had created this mess. He should let them finish cleaning it up. They'd already destroyed his memories and his grandmother's home as he knew it.

She was still waiting for an answer when he drew in a breath.

"Fine." He didn't want her to think she was off the hook, so he added, "We'll talk in the morning. There's going to be some ground rules."

"Okay." Her relief was visible as she nodded and clutched the shower curtain. "Thank you."

Christ. Now she was looking all doe-eyed and grateful. He didn't want that either. "Don't thank me. Just finish this shit and get the fuck out of my house as soon as you can."

He saw her expression wilting from his words. Good. Maybe now she'd finish even faster. Hate and fear—both powerful motivators.

His job done there, he turned and closed the door behind him. He needed that beer now more than ever.

CHAPTER EIGHT

Gabby couldn't see out of the rear window of her SUV from all the stuff, and her hands were shaking as she tried to steer out of the driveway.

She probably had no business being on the road like this but she had no choice.

Zach wanted her out and she hadn't been brave enough to disagree with him. How could she? He was completely in the right. She was a squatter.

A homeless squatter.

She'd have to rent a storage unit in the morning and get all of her stuff out before Zach threw it all into the road for the trash pickup. Moving her stuff by herself was going to take hours. And she was probably going to have to rent a truck to move the bigger stuff. And beg Amanda and Jasper to help her get the heavy furniture into the truck.

A truck. A storage unit. How much was all that stuff going to cost? Less than rent she reminded herself, which she no longer had to pay, being homeless and all.

She'd have to couch surf, and live by the good

graces of her best friend in the guest room. Or move to that horrible apartment building she'd seen. Or give up her hopes and dreams and move home to her parents' place.

Every one of those options sucked.

As the streetlights blurred before her eyes, she fought the tears and concentrated on the road ahead.

He'd been pissed. He'd been scary. Then he'd laughed at her. Amanda's big bad SEAL brother was frightening on a good day. But a laughing Zach was the most terrifying of all.

Is that what SEALs did before they killed someone with their bare hands? Laughed?

She'd told Amanda he wouldn't be happy with—

Darn it! Amanda.

Zach was probably going to call her. Gabby needed to get to her first and explain.

Nearly running off the road, she managed to get out her cell and call the number.

When Amanda answered, Gabby burst out with, "Has Zach called you tonight?"

"No. Stop worrying. I told you he's not going to be home for—"

Wrong!

"Don't answer your phone if he calls," Gabby cut off her friend.

"What? Why not?" she asked.

"Please, Amanda. I'm on my way to your house now. I have to explain something to you in person before you talk to Zach."

"Why are you so convinced Zach is going to call me tonight?"

"Because he's home. And he found me in his house. And he's really pissed."

"Well, then he can just be mad at me. I'm the one who hired you."

"No. I mean yes, there is that. But there's more."

"What more?" Amanda asked.

"Please, just trust me. I'll be there in half an hour. I'll explain everything when I get there. Just don't answer his calls until I do."

"All right. But he's really home? So soon?"

"Oh, yeah. He's home. Safe and sound." And looking as hot as he was angry.

Why did Mother Nature put such a mean man in such a beautiful package? It was really unfair to womankind.

Of course, maybe he was only mean to her. That was a distinct possibility.

If she ever had any chance of his getting over that little mishap in college well over a decade ago, it was gone now.

She just couldn't catch a break with this guy.

Maybe one day her damn heart would realize that it was a lost cause and stop fluttering every time someone even mentioned Zach's name.

Schoolgirl crushes on your best friend's brother rarely, if ever, worked out. And since he hated her, that was a certainty.

"He's texting me." Amanda's announcement brought Gabby's attention back to the call.

Gabby winced. "What's it say?"

"Call me. All caps. Two exclamation points."

Uh oh. That was bad.

"Amanda—"

"Gabby, stop. He'll get over it. I promise you. Besides, I hired you. I paid you. Redecorating his house while he was away was my idea and clearly my doing. Not yours."

All of Amanda's assurances might have made Gabby feel better if she hadn't seen that smoldering look in his eyes. And not the good kind of smolder either.

Not the kind you read about in romance novels right before the hero tosses the heroine onto the bed and has his way with her.

Oh no. This was the kind of look that said a volcano's worth of molten hate simmered inside him, just waiting for him to go off.

Then no one would be safe, particularly not Gabby, right there in the lava's path.

Amanda would be in the path of destruction too.

What if he was on the way to Amanda's house right now too? He had a long head start on her. She'd had to dry off and dress.

She couldn't risk Volcano Zach going off without at least trying to warn the villagers—er, make that Amanda. She couldn't wait to do this in person.

"Amanda, I have something to tell you."

There was the slightest pause. "All right."

"Zach might be mad about more than just the redecorating."

Another pause, longer this time. This one heavy with what she imagined was her friend's mingled dread and suspicion.

Finally, Amanda said, "Gabby, what did you do?"

"Um, so remember that time in college when he was in the shower?"

"Yes." Amanda stretched the word out in an even, measured tone.

Gabby drew in a deep breath. "So funny story . . ."

CHAPTER NINE

All Zach could think as he sat at his favorite drinking establishment in Coronado was that it was a good thing for Gabby that he had made plans with the team to meet at McP's Pub tonight.

If he hadn't, there was no way he would have left her there alone in his house.

Meanwhile, his text to his sister was still unanswered.

Scowling, he tossed the cell down onto the table where he could keep an eye on it and reached for his beer.

"Dude. It's our last team night at McP's before Compass and Hawk are gone. *Forever.*" Dutch stressed the word, as if Zach needed to be reminded that things would never be the same. "How about paying a little attention to your teammates and stop playing with your damn phone?"

"Fuck you. I'm paying attention." He just happened to also be checking his cell for a reply from Amanda, who was ignoring him. And pissing him off.

"Who are you trying to get a hold of, Z-man?

Tonight's lucky lady?" Justus asked with a waggle of his eyebrows.

"No. Eww." Zack cringed at the suggestion. "I'm trying to get a hold of my damn sister."

"*Eww* is right. Even T-Bone here wouldn't do his own sister." Smart-ass Rocket hooked a thumb at the other SEAL, earning him a deep frown from the large Louisiana boy in return.

"I'm not setting up a booty call, you perve." Zach scowled. "I'm trying to get her on the phone so I can yell at her."

"Yeah, that sounds about right." Hawk grinned.

"And why are you trying to yell at your sister," Nitro asked.

"Listen to what she did to me." Zach raised his empty bottle to get the waitress's attention. He was going to need more alcohol to get through this story without cracking his damn molars from clenching his jaw so hard.

"She hired her friend to redecorate my house while we were gone. The whole thing. Carpets are torn out. Walls are painted. Furniture is missing, I don't even know to where. And all my shit's been moved." Zach wrapped up the horror story with what he considered the worst part—that Gabby had messed with his stuff—but instead of the sympathy he was due, he got frowns.

"Why are you mad? That was nice of her," Nitro said.

"And I bet it's costing your sister a butt load of money to have your place redone too. And you're pissed? Dude, you're nuts." Dutch shook his head.

What the fuck? These men were like brothers to him. His friends. His teammates. Not Amanda's.

They were supposed to take his side, not his sister's. Even if they didn't agree with him.

They must not fully understand what was going on.

"You didn't hear the worst of it. I come home, straight from the base, first time I'm setting foot in my house since we left, and the damn interior decorator is in my fucking shower. I walked right in on her."

Seven sets of eyes were glued to him as the questions started flying from every single one of the guys.

"She naked?"

"She cute?"

"How old is she?"

"Blonde or brunette? I need a complete visual here."

"Yeah, we're going to need more details, Z-man."

"Please tell me you have one of those clear shower curtains."

"Why didn't you bring her here with you?"

He sighed, not about to attempt answering them all, even if he'd wanted to, which he didn't.

Zach glanced skyward, appreciating the outdoor patio at McP's more than usual as he looked to the heavens for patience.

The warm gentle breeze carried on it the promise of hot wings but the ambience was being ruined by his teammates and this damn topic of conversation.

Finally he let out a breath and braced himself to convince his brothers in arms they were fighting for the wrong side. "I didn't bring her with me because she's my sister's friend, *not mine*. And more importantly, there's a good chance she's got a screw loose."

"Wait." Hawk narrowed his eyes. "Is this Amanda's roommate from college?"

"Yeah." Zach gratefully reached for the frosty beer bottle the waitress had just set down.

"The Hawaiian chick who looks like she should be on a billboard for sunscreen?" Hawk continued.

"Wait. What's this now?" That comment had apparently gotten Rocket's attention. He perked right up, suddenly more interested in the conversation than watching the group of women who'd just sat nearby.

"Oh yeah. This chick is hot as hell." Hawk nodded to Rocket.

"How the hell do you know?" Zach asked Hawk, while trying not to admit anything to do with Gabby's hotness.

"You jerk." Hawk shook his head. "Don't you remember she was with your sister at that barbecue your parents threw that one year the team was actually in town and could take the day off for the fourth of July?"

Zach remembered. He'd tried to block her presence out at all the family events she'd been creeping around.

Apparently he'd successfully done so for this one . . . until damn Hawk brought it up.

He scowled and admitted, "Yeah, that's her."

"Man, I'd be happy to find her in my shower." Hawk shot Zach a glance. "I don't know why you look so miserable."

"No, you would not be happy to find her in your shower. The whole situation was just . . . weird." And surprisingly uncomfortable, even though he was on the preferred side of the shower curtain this time, as opposed to a dozen years ago in the dorm.

"So since it looks like Z-man here isn't going to offer up any of the tasty tidbits, we're going to have to rely on you, Hawk. So come on. Spill it. We need the deets." Justus rested his forearms on the table and leaned toward Hawk.

"And measurements," Compass added, waggling his eyebrows.

Zach groaned. Just when he thought it couldn't get any worse, this discussion had, unbelievably, taken a turn for the gutter. He might not like Gabby, but he liked the way this conversation was going even less. "Come on, guys. She's my little sister's best friend—"

Hawk cocked one brow high. "You mean your thirty-year-old married CPA *little* sister?"

There was a round of glares from the team, all directed at Zach.

"She's just turning twenty-nine. Not thirty," he mumbled.

"Sounds like she's not so *little* anymore, Z-man," Dutch commented, one brow high.

"Deets, Hawk," Justus said again. He pulled his mouth to one side as he shot Zach an amused glance. "Since Z-man is apparently incapable of appreciating the gorgeous naked woman in his own house."

Hawk's lips twitched, apparently enjoying the ribbing Zach was getting. "Let's just say the day I met her the weather was as hot as she was *and* there was a pool . . ."

A round of whoops went around the table.

"Gabby, and Amanda too—sorry, Z-man, but it's true—were both in bikinis," Hawk continued.

"That's what I'm talking about." T-Bone rubbed his hands together.

"And there was music." Hawk, who obviously was enjoying being the storyteller, dangled that detail and paused for the expected reaction from the team.

"Oh, yeah. Tell us more." Rocket leaned forward, while Zach leaned back and took another gulp of his beer.

There was no use fighting them when they got like this. He shouldn't bother trying to stop Hawk's story at this point. Well, except for the fact that Hawk's recap of the barbecue Zach had all but forgotten brought back too many unwelcome memories.

Memories of Gabby and Amanda joking around that day by the pool the summer before their senior year in college.

As much as he'd tried to ignore the thorn in his side that day, he'd noticed Gabby all right. She'd been facing away from him, standing on top of the damn diving board, doing a hula.

Yes, literally doing the hula. Or at least she had been trying to teach the dance to Amanda, who apparently had not been born with the hula gene and needed lots of tutoring.

But from his vantage point, all he could see was the sway of Gabby's hips. The curve that nipped in to her narrow waist. The fall of long dark hair over one shoulder like a veil over one round breast.

Hawk was right. There, like that with the single pink hibiscus flower she'd plucked from his mom's bush and tucked behind one ear, she could have stepped right off a billboard advertising suntan lotion.

A tropical beauty surreally out of place on the concrete deck of his parents' backyard pool.

Zach had done well at ignoring her until then. But between the cold beer and that hot view, parts of his body—one part in particular—had become laser focused on Gabby. He'd been forced to head to the bathroom and *handle* the growing situation before he embarrassed himself.

No one else had seen, but he knew what had happened and he'd never stop being pissed at himself over it.

His parents sold that house a couple of years ago—right after his grandma had died. They'd moved to a retirement community on a golf course in Arizona, but he'd never forget that pool. And Hawk, still regaling the guys with a blown up retelling of the events of that day, obviously wasn't about to let Zach try.

Finally, Zach's phone rang—or rather the obnoxious song he'd assigned as the ringtone for his so often annoying sister sounded.

Baby shark, doo-doo, doo-doo doo-doo . . .

The ringtone elicited a round of groans from the men seated at the table.

"Dude! What the fuck?" T-Bone glared at the cell as if he was considering squashing it like a bug beneath his meaty fist.

Scowling, Nitro shot Zach a glare. "Shit, man. Now that fucking song is gonna be stuck in my head for days."

"I don't know. I kinda like it." Dutch shrugged. His comment momentarily redirected the team's wrath toward him and away from Zach.

"Sorry." Cringing, Zach snatched the cell and swiped the screen to answer the call. Raising the cell to his ear, he said, "About time you got back to me."

"Me! What about you?" Amanda lobbed the question back at him. "If anyone is uncommunicative in this family, it's you. When were you going to tell me you were home from the front?"

He rolled his eyes. "I wasn't *on the front*, as you call it."

And he would have gotten around to telling her he was home after he'd decompressed for a day or two. At least that had been his plan until it was shot to hell by little Miss Shower Curtain.

Amanda wouldn't understand what it was like to re-acclimate to normal civilian home life after being deployed for months. Since she'd never get it, he didn't bother trying to explain.

Instead he moved on to the issue uppermost in his mind. "Don't be a smart ass. You have a lot of explaining to do. Such as your friend living in my damn house while I was gone."

"Don't exaggerate. She wasn't living there. Well, at least not until yesterday."

Zach's eyes popped wide. "You knew? And you have no problem with it?"

The team's conversation at the table was getting in the way of Zach being able to completely concentrate on his call.

His sister was tricky. She could talk circles around anyone anytime. He'd need all his faculties to debate her and make sure she didn't get away with anything.

He stood and made his way toward the patio wall where he could hear better. The street noise was quieter than the group of SEALs into their second round.

"Gabby had a perfectly good explanation. It was all a misunderstanding and honestly, given how much work she's done and how little money she'd take for it, you should be grateful. You owe her," Amanda proclaimed.

"I owe her?" He let out a snort, but decided to move on to the bigger subject—Amanda hiring Gabby in the first place. "What were you thinking turning my place upside down while I was away?"

"I was thinking you might like coming home to a house that reflects who you are, and not one that looks like an eighty-year old woman has lived there since nineteen-fifty-six."

He drew in a breath. He happened to like the way it was. It was comfortable. He was used to it. And now it was all gone and God only knew what kind of modern shit Gabby was planning on moving in. He was going to have to find out. Maybe it wasn't too late to get everything back.

"Amanda, you should have asked me first."

"If I had you wouldn't have let me do it."

"Exactly. But instead you let her toss all of Grandma's stuff."

She paused and he braced for another argument. Finally, she said, "I'm sorry."

The apology, and the sincerity with which it was delivered, took him off guard.

He drew in a breath, feeling bad for not appreciating her gift, even if he hadn't wanted it in the first place. "It's okay. I know you meant well."

"She's going to finish."

He let out a laugh. "I'm not sure I want her to finish."

Taking his truck to the furniture store where he could pick his own stuff sounded like the safer bet. It would cost him but at least the choice would be his.

"Please, Zach. I've seen her plans. It's going to be perfect. I promise. And if you don't like it, I'll help you redo it all and pay for it."

He didn't like accepting anything from his sister, certainly not money. He was the older sibling. He was supposed to take care of her, not the other way around.

"Please . . ." she repeated. "Gabby is here crying her eyes out she's so upset that you're mad."

"I doubt that." Zach knew one thing about Amanda—she wasn't above exaggerating the truth to get her way.

"Don't be a hater. She didn't want to take the job. She warned me you'd be mad and I didn't listen, so if you're mad at anyone, it should be me. Not her. Let her finish the job, Zach."

A feeling of dread riding him, Zach drew in a breath and made probably the worst decision of his life. "All right. She can finish. But she has to move all her shit out of my garage."

He'd peeked inside and it looked like, crammed in there with a few of his own prized possessions including the big screen television, was what must be all of Gabby's belongings that didn't fit in her car.

"She will. I'm coming over tomorrow after work with a rental truck to help her move it all to a storage unit."

He had a bad feeling Amanda would be paying for at least part of that endeavor out of guilt. And he'd just end up helping them load all the shit anyway because there was no way two women were loading a moving truck while he sat on his ass and watched them.

He groaned, about to dig his own grave deeper. "No. Don't bother. It can stay in the garage. For now. But it all goes the minute she finds a permanent place to live. And that had better not be in your guestroom," he warned.

"It won't be. She's looking for a place. And thank you, Zach. I knew buried real deep down there was a good guy inside you somewhere."

"Watch it, sis. I can still change my mind."

"You could, but you won't." There was a smile in her voice. "Love you, bro. Oh, and Gabby will be there early-early. So don't be naked in the shower or anything when she gets there."

A growl was his response to that little joke. "Good night, Amanda."

"Night, Zach. Love you."

"Yeah, love you too." Rolling his eyes at how his sister had somehow managed to get her way once again, he disconnected the call and headed back to the table.

It seemed he'd be waking up to Gabby in the morning, whether he liked it or not. He sat and reached for his beer. He was going to need it.

CHAPTER TEN

The sun was just a hint of a peachy glow on the horizon when Gabby pulled her SUV next to Zach's truck parked in his driveway.

Just the sight of his vehicle was enough to give her heart palpitations—and not the good kind like she used to get when she caught a glimpse of him without his shirt by his parents' pool.

This was the last place she wanted to be right now. The thrill of finishing this house had been totally trampled by the reappearance of the man who owned it.

They could have made a new emoji out of Zach's expression yesterday when he'd caught her there. It could be called *mean scary frowny-faced man.*

Sitting in the driver's seat and staring at the house wasn't productive. Every moment she procrastinated in the driveway was another delay in getting this job done, and finishing fast was more critical now than ever.

She hated feeling like she was intruding but she had no choice. Drawing in a breath she opened the door and stepped down. Everything she needed was already here since she'd been planning on working—and living—there before Zach's untimely reappearance.

At the front door, she paused. She still had the key, which she supposed she should return to Amanda before Zach called the cops on her. Should she use it now? It was really early.

Would Zach be madder that she let herself in or that she woke him up at the crack of dawn ringing the bell? It was a tough call. A paralyzing decision. She was so afraid of pissing this man off further she couldn't move.

Fuck it. She had work to do. Amanda had told him she'd be here today early to finish. She'd heard the phone conversation. He'd been warned.

She slid the key into the lock and as quietly as she could, let herself inside. Creeping through the dark house made her feel even more like a criminal until she got to the door leading to the garage.

Slipping into the garage, she turned on the lights so she could get to work. It felt like she'd reached sanctuary, even though it looked more like a storage unit at the moment, filled with most of her apartment's contents.

Luckily, she'd sanded everything outside in the driveway yesterday—before her shower and before Zach had kicked her out of his house.

This morning, she could start painting all of her treasures.

A couple of coats and the little wooden table would be ready to put in place in the master bedroom as a nightstand. No one would ever guess its humble origin as street side trash.

Same with the wood shutters she'd found by the dumpster behind the Home Depot. They'd been tossed because the wood on the bottom had splintered but Gabby didn't care. They'd be the headboard for Zach's bedroom.

The new queen-sized mattress and box spring with the free bonus frame she'd had delivered would completely hide the damage on the bottom of the shutters.

With the dresser that had already been in the house, the bedroom would be complete. She could get that put together today and hopefully appease Zach. Once he saw how great it looked, he'd have faith in her. He had to. Maybe. Hopefully.

Grrr. This man! All he did was make her insecure. Or more insecure than usual. It wasn't like she needed much of a push to doubt herself.

Prying open the can of fresh white paint, Gabby got to work.

Normally she'd have the radio blasting while she painted but she didn't want to disturb Zach. Even when he wasn't scowling at her, he could ruin her fun.

He'd probably enjoy knowing that.

The thought had her shaking her head. The man didn't deserve this beautiful new headboard she'd envisioned.

She'd been wanting to do a project like this for her own place for months and if the situation had been different, there was a good chance these shutters would have found their way into her bedroom rather than Zach's.

But as it was, with her being temporarily homeless and all, it made more sense to use them for Zach's. Besides the fact they'd be perfect with the new sea glass blue paint in his master bedroom.

She'd definitely have to take lots of pictures of her completed design for the blog. She'd be damned if she let this great project go completely to waste on a man who would probably never appreciate it.

The first swipe of paint across the top of the little table had the excitement growing within her, just like it always did when she took the old and turned it into something outstanding.

The next swipe and the next showed even more how beautiful the scarred old table would become.

Just because something was a little worn around the edges didn't mean it stopped being useful. How could the homeowner have not seen the value in this?

The curving shape of the legs. The piecrust detail edging the top. That it wasn't made out of pressboard beneath veneer like so much of the furniture was nowadays. They didn't make solid wood tables like this anymore.

She brushed on a fairly thick coat of the paint and thanks to the wide brush she covered the table with the first coat quickly and moved on to the shutters.

This part was therapeutic—getting closer to the end product.

Then again, she liked the dumpster diving just as much. The thrill of the hunt. The discovery of something amazing. Taking something and turning it into something else.

"I want adventure in the great wide somewhere . . ." She sang softly turning the shutters around so she could paint the metal brackets she'd screwed in to hold the three individual panels together.

Turning, she reached to move the paint closer and jumped at the sudden sight of Zach in the doorway.

"Good morning." He looked too amused at her expense as he stood there shirtless with the hint of a smirk on his lips.

She yanked her gaze off his bare chest. "You scared me."

"I scared you?" He lifted one brow. "You're the one who came creeping in the front door at dawn. And then proceeded to bang around in here for the past half hour."

"I wasn't banging." She pouted, apparently destined to always be on this man's bad side.

"Only singing." Those lips twitched again before he lifted his mug to that smart mouth of his and sipped the coffee.

Boy, did that coffee smell good. Now that he had the door to the kitchen open she'd gotten a full whiff of a fresh brewed pot.

As if he'd read her mind—or maybe had just seen her looking longingly at his beverage—he lifted the mug to her. "Want coffee?"

She somehow felt like his offer was a trap. Some kind of trick. As if he'd wait for her to say *yes, please* and start to salivate before he said, *sorry, you can't have any.*

Finally the craving took over. Not to mention the fact she'd slept like crap last night—no surprise there—and she could use the caffeine boost.

Gabby gathered her nerve, braced herself and said, "If that's a sincere offer, I'd love some coffee."

Frowning, he pulled his mouth to one side. "Of course it's a sincere offer. Jesus."

Mumbling, he turned and went back into the kitchen, letting the door shut behind him. Which meant she once again felt like an intruder as she opened the door, peeked through still not convinced this wasn't a trick, and finally stepped inside.

Zach faced the counter, giving her the perfect view of his wide shoulders and the well defined muscles of his back that narrowed to his waist.

His muscles worked beneath his smooth tanned skin as he reached for a high shelf to take down a mug. "At least you didn't fuck with my cabinets."

"I tried to disturb as little of your stuff as possible."

He turned to face her, that brow cocked high again. He didn't comment as he handed her the mug and said, "Milk is in the fridge. Sugar in the canister on the counter."

So many things she could have said.

That she was impressed he'd been home for less than twelve hours and had already stocked up on food—or at least milk for his coffee. That she knew where the sugar was because she'd borrowed some just last week when the coffee she'd grabbed at the gas station on the way over was too strong.

She didn't say any of that. Instead, she said, "Thanks."

He lifted one shoulder. "It's nothing."

Zach was wrong. His not throwing her out, and his giving her coffee, was definitely something. More than she'd expected after their reunion last night.

"You drink it black?" he asked, sounding surprised.

He watched her, standing there with the mug in one hand, paralyzed with having him here in the space that had been solely hers for weeks.

She finally managed a small shake of her head.

"Yeah, didn't think so." He pushed off the counter

and padded toward the fridge and for the first time she realized he was barefoot.

She'd been too busy looking at his chest. And how the waist of his jeans hung just low enough for her to see that oh so sexy vee and that dusting of hair. The happy trail leading to . . .

She drew her mind and her eyes off what had mesmerized her now that he faced the fridge, those two dimples at the bottom of his back just at the top of his butt cheeks.

He turned back with the milk in his hand and held it over her mug, waiting for an answer to his unspoken offer.

"Yes, please."

He tipped the carton and splashed milk into her mug, then returned the carton to the shelf on the fridge.

As she stood there cradling the brimming mug, he moved back to the counter and pulled a spoon out of the drawer. He carried it and the open sugar canister to where she stood in the middle of the room.

"How many?"

"Two . . . and a half."

He leveled an amused gaze on her and scooped the white granules into her mug, even stirring it for her.

"Thank you," she said again.

"You're welcome."

As he turned away to drop the spoon in the sink, she managed to take her first long swallow of the coffee.

Her eyes closed as she enjoyed the hot sweet liquid filling her mouth. When she opened them again it was to find Zach watching her.

"Good?" he asked.

"Yes. So good."

To her surprise, he actually laughed. "Amanda's coffee sucks."

She bit her lip but finally nodded. "It really does."

"I swear, I don't know what she does to it," he agreed.

Enjoying this rare moment of camaraderie she said, "She makes it too strong. It's like . . . ugh."

Look at them, talking civilly. At least for four sentences. Now they were back to awkward silence as they both sipped their coffee.

Finally she decided she needed to acknowledge that he'd let her back in his home at all. "Thank you, for letting me finish."

He lifted one shoulder. "I figured it was the best chance I had for getting something to sit on. As it was I had to carry in the mattress from the garage to sleep on last night."

Her eyes widened as she hissed in a breath. "I'm so sorry. I forgot I didn't have them set up the bedframe because I hadn't painted that room yet when it was delivered."

She didn't mention that she'd just slept on the floor the one night she'd stayed here before he'd caught her. She'd gotten done moving all of her stuff so late that night, the pile of comforters had been the best she could do.

"It's okay. It's done. Nice mattress, by the way. Comfortable."

Again she watched him, looking for sarcasm or mocking but finding none.

"There's a one year guarantee that if you don't like it I can return it."

"No, it's good."

"I would have gotten you a king but I measured and the room was so small it would have left you no space—"

"It's fine. I'm used to way worse than an eighteen-inch thick pillow-top queen-size. I'm gonna need sheets though."

Gabby cringed. "Sorry. I ordered a set. They're in the garage in the shipping box."

He nodded. "Nice to know some of the stuff in there is mine."

"Thank you for that too—letting me keep my stuff here until I get a place."

"Sure."

He certainly was agreeable today. She supposed she should by grateful. And offer to help make the place more livable for him. "I can help you hang your television back up today."

He shook his head. "Already done."

"Really? By yourself?" She spun and looked at the living room wall and there it was.

It was so damn big she'd had to have Amanda and Jasper help her take it down so she could paint.

"By myself." He nodded. "I was motivated."

Apparently. Although his muscles did look big enough to handle the sixty-inch monster.

Thoughts of inches and what else might be a big monster on Zach had her cheeks heating.

She hid behind her mug and sipped.

Did he always walk around without a shirt?

All day long? Or just in the morning? She'd have to be sure to do all her work here early in the morning just in case.

"So, what were you doing out there?" He tipped

his chin toward the door to the garage.

"Painting."

He rolled his eyes. "I saw that. And even if I hadn't, the paint all over you would have been a big clue."

Gabby glanced down at herself while she touched her face. She thought she'd kept clean.

He tapped a spot on his own elbow. Gabby glanced down and saw the white line on the back of her forearm from wrist to elbow. She must have leaned on the edge of the shutters.

"I meant, what are you painting?" he asked, once she'd noticed and decided to ignore the paint.

This was treacherous terrain. If she'd finished the furniture, moved it in and staged the room to look like her vision, she might have had a chance. But there was no way Zach was going to like what she'd chosen now while it was half done sitting in the garage only half-transformed.

"Can I show you?" she asked.

It was a long shot, but maybe, with her leading him, he would be able to see her vision.

The likelihood of this big bad scowly-faced Navy SEAL appreciating her trash to treasure obsession was slim, but she was going to try anyway. Call her a sucker for lost causes.

Hell, her whole career had felt like a lost cause until just recently and, aside from a few bumps, things were still going along nicely. Or would be once she finished this job and got to Tijuana to buy those tiles . . . but that was a job for another day.

Today, her focus was on Amanda's pessimistic brother.

He watched her for so long she was wondering if

he was going to reply to her request or not.

Finally, he tipped his head in a nod. "Sure."

Surprised by his answer, in spite of her hopes, she jumped to lead him to her makeshift workshop, leaving the mug behind on the counter so she would have two hands to conduct her tour.

He followed her through the doorway, even though on some level she still expected him to slam and lock the door behind her.

First she went to the table. "I was thinking this would look nice next to your bed—to use as a nightstand. It's got a drawer," she added as extra incentive for him to like it.

He watched her but didn't comment.

She continued, "The white will be a nice complement to the blue wall color." The color she hoped he didn't hate.

Still he said nothing. Just stood there holding his mug and alternating between looking at her and the table.

Maybe his silence was a good thing.

Going with that theory, she moved to the shutters. "And these are going to be the headboard for your bed. Again, the white will match the bedside table and go nice against the walls."

"Where's my grandmother's bed?" he asked, his tone low with what could only be described as a warning.

"Right here." She scrambled to the opposite side of the garage.

When she got halfway there, she realized he couldn't see the headboard behind all the stuff from her apartment stacked in front of it.

She glanced back. "It's back there. I was going to

put that in the guest bedroom since it's only a full size. I'd thought you'd want a bigger mattress for your bedroom. I can move that back inside and into the guest room today if you want. It's a beautiful old piece."

Lips pressed together, his only answer was a nod.

"Okay, so um, this . . ." She moved back to her work area. "This is going to be a charging station. I was going to leave it unfinished since I think the wine logo is kind of cool but I can paint it if you want. See, you open it and plug in your devices but you don't have to look at all the cords."

Gabby lifted the lid of the wooden wine box to demonstrate.

"I just have to drill a hole in the back for the surge protector power strip cord. I already bought one. It's got six plugs and four USB ports . . ." She watched him to see if he was following her explanation—or scowling.

Amazingly, his face showed no expression. Wondering if that was a good thing or a bad thing, Gabby decided to forge ahead.

"I was going to put it on top of these legs and stand it in front of the outlet in the wall in the living room, by the hall doorway. But if you want it somewhere else . . ." She let the sentence trail off, wondering if he was going to give her any sort of feedback at all, and deciding if she really wanted it or not.

"Where's my golf ball and scorecard?" he asked.

"Inside the hall closet in a box of accessories. Safe. I promise. Nice job, by the way. Hole-in-one. That's impressive."

He looked anything but impressed with her. She

drew in a breath.

"Where's the sofa?" he asked.

"At the reupholsterer. It had good bones but the fabric was shot. And dated." God she hoped he liked what she'd chosen.

Amanda had loved it. Unfortunately, Amanda wasn't the one who had to live with it.

The more she talked the more she realized how ill advised this whole surprise decorating project had been.

She dared to raise her gaze to him. He nodded. Not much, by way of feedback, but she'd take it.

Feeling brave—a nod was definitely better than some of the other ways he could have responded—she gathered her courage and dared to ask, "What do you think?"

Braced for the answer, she waited.

Finally, he said, "I think you and Amanda were fucking insane to do this while I was away without my knowing."

"I know. I agree. And I'm sorry."

He drew in a breath. "But you're lucky. Because I don't hate what you've done."

Her eyes widened. "Really?"

"Yeah." He tipped his head toward the shutters. "You put that together yourself?"

"Yes." She nodded with enthusiasm. "It was really easy. I just had to screw in some brackets to hold the shutters together then paint them. The whole headboard cost under ten dollars."

"What?" His brows drew low.

Uh oh. Was this good shock or bad shock? Either way, it was time to come clean about the source of his new furniture. At least partially.

"Um, yeah. The store was getting rid of the shutters."

"So they had them on sale for ten bucks?" he asked.

"Actually, they were, um, free." She swallowed hard, hoping he'd leave it at that, with her little half-truth being the last of this discussion.

"Why would they be free?" he asked.

This she could answer. "Well, the bottom was all splintered. I think they must have fallen and it messed up the wood. But I just used some wood putty and sand paper, then painted them white and once they're behind the bed you'll never know they were damaged."

"Humph." Was that lifted brow a sign he was impressed?

Encouraged, she went on. "I saw a shutter headboard like this being sold at one of the big stores for over six hundred dollars."

He bobbed his head, and yes, that was approval she saw from him. Miracles never ceased.

"So, if you approve of the direction I took, I was hoping to get most of this stuff finished and moved back inside today."

"All right. Let me know if you need help carrying the big stuff."

"Oh, okay. Thanks."

"No problem." He turned and then was gone, leaving Gabby in a state of shock that soon turned to euphoria and a smile she couldn't control.

If she could win over Zach, she could do anything!

CHAPTER ELEVEN

"I'm waiting for my apology."

"Oh, are you now? And for what would I be apologizing?" Zach asked his sister as he set his dinner plate in the sink with the one hand not holding the cell phone.

"Gabby came home from your place and said you liked what she's doing with the decor."

There were so many things wrong with his sister's statement, Zach didn't know where to begin.

First and foremost was that the house belonging to Amanda and her husband was not Gabby's *home*. And it pissed him off to no end to see his sister being taken advantage of by her friend like this.

He decided to say just that. "Your house is not Gabby's home."

"It is for as long as I say it is. And I told you, it's only temporary. Her building sold and the new asshole landlord doubled the rent and kicked out everyone who wouldn't pay the increase."

This was all news to Zach. He knew she'd been squatting at his place, but she never told him why.

"Didn't she have a lease?" he asked.

"She did, but it was up."

"And he gave her no notice? That's illegal." Zach frowned.

"He gave her thirty days, but that's not the point."

Zach considered that exactly the point. Thirty days was plenty of time for Gabby to have found another place to live—if she hadn't been planning to squat at his house. He reverted back to his original opinion of the situation.

Amanda continued, "The point is that you, who were so against making any changes to your house, like it."

Even though it was true and he did like what she'd done, he couldn't force himself to admit it. Definitely not to his meddling sister.

"Nope. I never said I liked it. I said I didn't hate it."

Amanda snorted. "Same thing when it comes to you."

He narrowed his eyes, feeling like he might have been insulted, but not sure. "Whatever. The point remains you shouldn't have done it behind my back."

"I've apologized for that."

Had she really? He tried to review their recent conversations. Yes, she might have actually said the words, *I'm sorry,* but he wasn't in the mood to give her credit for it now.

Gabby had apologized though. He remembered that clearly and he respected her for it. She might be a lunatic—that fact had yet to be disproved in his mind—but at least she could admit when she was wrong.

Unlike his sister.

"Was there a reason for this call, other than your vain hope that I'd be apologizing to you? Which isn't going to happen, by the way."

"Yes, actually, there is. Have you ever driven across the Tijuana border?" Amanda asked.

"Yes. Why?" It had been years but a person really couldn't live in San Diego without having made at least one trip across the border.

"Is it dangerous?"

"Why?" he asked again since she hadn't answered him the first time. Suspicious, he added, "You're not going."

"No. It's not me."

"Then who?"

"Gabby."

That figured. If she wasn't causing trouble for him or his sister, she was getting into it by herself.

He sighed, not liking the idea of her going either, in spite of the fact he had really no connection to her. "I wouldn't call Tijuana dangerous, per se, but I wouldn't consider it safe either. It's a lot better now than it used to be. But either way, it's still a foreign country. You've got to be smart and careful."

"Okay. I'll tell her."

Zach shook his head. Sadly, he doubted Gabby's ability to be either smart or careful. But what could he do? He had no say over Gabby's life.

But he did have something to say about how Amanda lived her life. "Just tell me you're really not going with her and aren't just lying to me."

"I'm not going. I have to work that day or I would be going and you wouldn't be able to stop me."

He cocked a brow at her comment. "I might not be able to, but I bet your husband could."

Zach wasn't above tattling to his brother-in-law if it meant keeping his sister safe.

Amanda laughed. "Oh, Zach. You're so funny that you believe that. Love you. Gotta go." She disconnected before he could protest and left him shaking his head.

He'd definitely be telling Jasper to keep an eye on his wild child sister. Zach did exactly that in a text before he carried his small bag of garbage out to the bin in the garage.

On the way back to the kitchen, he paused to evaluate Gabby's projects.

To her credit, she'd stayed pretty much out of his way all day today. But before she left, she'd popped inside to give him an update.

She'd proclaimed her painting projects not dry enough to move inside before she left for the day so he still had no table in his bedroom.

He paused to touched one finger to the shutter and felt that the paint was now dry.

Squatting down, he checked out the bottom, where she'd said the shutters had been damaged. He could barely see the repairs she'd made. Standing again, he evaluated the piece from the back. He could just see the outline of the small metal braces beneath a coat of paint.

The damn girl had even painted the back of the headboard that would be against the wall. He couldn't help but admire her diligence and work ethic—even if admiration was a strange sensation for him when it came to Gabby.

He stepped carefully around the clutter in his formerly bare garage and moved to the wine box. He lifted the lid.

She'd set the power strip inside and drilled a round hole in the back just big enough for the plug to slip through.

He would have never in a million years pegged Gabby as a woman who could use power tools. Or as one who would ever want to. But she had proven she was both.

Letting the box's lid close he turned for the kitchen door.

Inside, even with a cold beer open on the counter waiting for him to drink it, something had him instead opening a new search browser on his cell phone and punching in her name.

Her blog came up in the search results. He hit the link and the site loaded.

There was a lot there. Apparently she liked to write as much as she liked to talk. He scrolled through a few pictures and then saw a menu of recent posts.

The one titled *Dumpster Diving* had him clicking to open it and there was a picture of Gabby standing proudly in front of a dumpster to take a selfie with a stack of wooden shutters. The caption read, *Today's find*.

"I'll be damned." Zach let out a soft laugh.

Even though she'd led him to believe the store had given her the damaged shutters, the little wench had made his headboard out of literal trash she'd found in the dumpster behind the store.

Rather than being mad at her for skirting the truth, he couldn't help but be a little impressed.

She had balls. He'd give her that.

He was starting to see why she and his sister had been close for so many years. Amanda would have no problem doing something as brazen. Although, as far as he knew, Amanda didn't have the vision or the skills to turn garbage into home décor that didn't look like she'd fished it out of a dumpster.

Suddenly, he didn't want to wait to see how it would all look inside.

Heading back out to the garage he grabbed the table and the charger box and carried them both inside. He went right back out for the headboard and then made another trip for his toolbox.

Half an hour later, he evaluated the headboard he'd bolted to the bedframe and the table next to it.

Gabby had located the sheets she'd bought and though she'd wanted to put them on the bed for him, he'd told her he would take care of it. She'd chosen a crisp gray and white pinstripe design that looked pretty good with the new white comforter and the pale blue walls.

All put together, it looked damn good . . . not that he was inclined to tell her that.

Inspiration struck and Zach headed back to the garage where he'd spotted one of his grandmother's lamps. He carried the brass lamp back inside and set it on the night table.

He didn't know what Gabby had planned but his addition didn't look half bad. It might look even better with a new shade . . .

Inspired, he went back out to look for more stuff he could move in.

He found a box of his grandmother's books. He carried that inside and started setting them back on the freshly painted bookshelves, where they'd been since he'd visited her as a child.

Then he decided to find his golf ball and scorecard since he didn't trust Gabby not to have lost them.

That led to him searching for some other things he'd accumulated over the years but had never unpacked when he'd moved in.

The bible his grandmother had given him, embossed with his name and the date that he'd graduated from boot camp.

The bullet—in a clear plastic box for preservation—that Nitro had dug out of him on the transport during the exfil from a mission he'd never be able to talk about with anyone besides the team, but would never forget.

The tiny ship in a bottle Amanda had given him one year for Christmas. He set it all on the shelves, his adult memories intermingled with those of his childhood.

By the time he was done moving things around he was down to the last beer in the six-pack.

He glanced at the time and was shocked at how late it was. What was wrong with him? Decorating. Jeesh. One day in the proximity of that girl and he'd lost his mind.

Good thing the team couldn't see him. He'd never hear the end of the teasing.

CHAPTER TWELVE

Gabby snuck in through the front door just as she had the day before, except this time everything was different. In the early morning light streaming in she could see that clearly.

There were books and accessories on the bookshelves in the living room. And in front of it was the old La-Z-Boy chair she'd been planning on tossing once Zach gave her permission to.

Just to the right of the eyesore of the worn recliner, plugged into the wall was her charging station.

Frowning she resisted the urge to flip on all the lights to see what else Zach had done to her carefully laid out plans while she wasn't looking.

"Good morning." His voice came from the kitchen, followed by the sound of the garage door slamming.

She spun and saw Zach holding the old coffee table she'd also been hoping to ditch in the yard sale she still had yet to pitch to Zach.

Judging by how he was carrying it into the living

room, she had a feeling the item was going to be staying.

"Good morning," she finally said. "I, uh, see you were busy last night."

He grinned, an actual happy expression, which threw her further off kilter. "Yeah. It was kind of fun arranging everything. And don't tell my sister that or I'll just deny it."

"I wouldn't dream of it." Damn, this was one contingency she hadn't planned on—Zach being into decorating and having his own plan that ran counter to hers.

She drew in a breath and was just trying to figure out how to deal with this when he plopped the coffee table down next to the armchair, where it was much too low to function as a side table and turned to her.

"Come into the bedroom."

All those years she'd wished Zach would say exactly those words to her as her school girl self drooled over the thought of him . . . Now that he'd finally said them she was dreading what she'd find in there.

What havoc had he wreaked with her design plan in the master bedroom? She couldn't even imagine.

She followed behind as Zach swung the door wide.

Holding her breath she stepped inside and let it out in a whoosh. He'd brought in the headboard and the little white side table she'd painted.

The one place he'd gone rogue was adding a brass lamp to the table, but she actually liked it.

The rich shine of the brass somehow complimented the airy white and blue décor. And the heavy item gave the room a masculine feel. With a new shade, it would look perfect.

He said, "I figure I'll pick up a lampshade somewhere."

Gabby whipped her head to stare at Zach as he voiced the exact thought she'd been having. "Um, yeah. I agree."

"Where should I go to buy one of those?" he asked. "A lampshade."

Now he wanted to go shopping? What had happened?

Wherever he'd been recently, he must have gotten hit on the head. Or had some sort of near death experience, because this man was nothing like the Zach she'd known for years.

He was still watching her, waiting for an answer. What was the question again? Oh, yeah. A lampshade.

"I can pick one up for you."

He shook his head. "That's okay. I don't mind going."

"Okay. The lighting stores all have them, but so do any of the big chain superstores. Even Home Depot has a lighting aisle, if you want to check there first. They've got some nice options."

He nodded, looking intrigued with his impending shopping trip to Home Depot for lampshades.

She glanced back at the bed, neatly made as if it wasn't the crack of dawn and most people would be lolling around under the covers still.

This must be SEAL training because it certainly wasn't nature or nurture. Gabby had been Amanda's roommate for four years in college and she could count the number of times that girl had made her bed on two hands.

She shot Zach a glance. Since he was being so

agreeable she decided to push her luck. "So, I guess you like the headboard then?"

He cocked a brow high. "Fishing for a compliment?"

Her cheeks warmed. How could such an oaf be so perceptive? "No. Looking for feedback as a design professional."

He sniffed out a laugh at her distinction. "Yeah, I like it. It's cool."

Wow. They'd come a long way for him to admit he liked something she did.

He must have seen in her expression how excited she was because he leveled a glare on her and said, "Don't get too cocky. I know you were planning on tossing my favorite chair."

No, she wasn't. At least not without asking first.

"What makes you think that?" she asked, feigning as much innocence as she could muster.

"The sticky note that said 'toss' on it."

Shit, she'd forgotten about that. So much for trying to be extra organized. All it did was come back to bite her in the butt.

"I believe I put a question mark after that word. And if it is your favorite chair, then you definitely should keep it," she said.

"Even though you hate it." He watched her, waiting.

"Yes. Even though I really do." She couldn't help but admit the truth. "But it's your house and it needs to reflect you."

"I wouldn't have said that foo-foo wine crates turned into charging stations and tiny white tables reflected me, but now that it's all in here, I actually don't mind it."

Pride warmed her. And hope. If she could please Zach, who they had to treat as a hostile client, she really had a shot of making a go in this profession.

"But—" His single word had her hopes and dreams screeching to a halt. She waited until he finally said, "Please, for the love of God, do not get the rest of my furniture from out of a dumpster."

Her eyes flew wide. "You know about that?"

Had Amanda told him? That little—*grrr.* That was the last time she confided a secret in her.

"Yes, I know about that. And it would have been nice if you'd told me the truth, instead of me having to read it on your blog."

"What?" Her eyes widened.

As realization hit a smile threatened to break out wide.

Sometime last night in between his foray into decorating, Zachary Brown, the man she'd had a crush on for all of her adult life, had googled her. And he'd taken the time to read her blog.

"Stop." There was warning in his tone. "It's no big deal. I stumbled upon it accidentally."

He might be trying to act casual, but he looked as if he was sorry he'd ever brought it up.

"Mmm, hmm." Her smile finally broke free.

He sighed. "I'm having coffee. If you want some I suggest you stop grinning like a fool and come to the kitchen."

Somehow even his gruff rudeness took on a whole new light this morning.

A new day had dawned, in more ways than one. It kind of made her sad this job was almost over.

A few paintings to put back on the walls. The guest room furniture still had to come back in from the garage—if Zach hadn't already done that during his insomniac decorating—and then as soon as the sofa was back from the reupholster she'd be done.

That was probably for the best.

Besides her needing to get far away from Zach before her hormones took over, she had to get the coffee shop done so she could get paid for it. Tile— gorgeous and hand painted and a bargain price— awaited her in Tijuana.

Zach planting the mug of coffee in front of her brought her out of her own head. "With milk and sugar, just how you like it."

He'd fixed her coffee for her. How could a man be such an ass sometimes, and at others be so . . . perfect?

Surprised, and feeling the warmth and excitement spreading through her, she said, "Thanks."

Her crush was back in full force. And her eighteen-year old girl feelings for him, combined with the desire of a twenty-nine year old woman who hadn't had sex in forever, made for a dangerous combination.

"Let me get that out of the way." Zach leaned forward to reach past her and grab for the empty beer bottle on the counter at the same time Gabby reached for the coffee mug.

The clunk of their foreheads was only avoided because of Zach's quick reflexes.

She felt the weight of his hand on her shoulder just before cranial impact. But even though they didn't collide, they were still just a breath away.

"Sorry." He exhaled and the warmth of his breath brushed across her cheek.

He smelled of minty toothpaste and somewhere in

the back of her mind a voice—maybe more than one voice—chanted, *kiss him, kiss him, kiss him.*

Maybe she needed therapy. Hearing voices in her head couldn't be good. And, admittedly, wanting to kiss the man who had loathed her since college was also a problem.

Loathe at first sight. That about covered his feelings for her since that first meeting in the dorms.

Gabby swallowed and leaned back, out of the danger zone where Zach's tempting mouth remained.

"My fault. I'm the klutz between us. You're—" Where was she going to go with this sentence? Uh, oh.

His green and gold-flecked eyes remained focused on her. "I'm what?"

A big gorgeous SEAL with reflexes like a panther and a body like Adonis and . . . She cleared her throat.

"And you're clearly not a klutz." She snatched her mug off the counter and leaned back farther, adding for good measure, "I've seen Amanda trip over her own feet so it must be all that military training you've had."

One corner of his mouth quirked up in a crooked smile. "Must be."

CHAPTER THIRTEEN

"Thanks for inviting me." Zach stepped into Amanda's house, a bottle of wine in his hand—his contribution since she was having him over for dinner.

He was no heathen thanks to his grandmother's impeccably good manners that she somehow had managed to instill in him over the years.

Did he intend on drinking the wine? Fuck, no.

Was he counting on his brother-in-law having beer in the house? Hell, yes.

Jasper had better have a stocked fridge because Zach had a feeling he was going to need a couple brews to get through tonight. For the time being—and he sincerely hoped it wouldn't be for long—Gabby was still staying here at Amanda's. That meant dinner with Amanda and Jasper would most certainly include Gabby.

Yes, over the past few days Gabby had gone from a thorn in his side to more of a splinter in his finger.

But a splinter was still plenty annoying.

And even more annoying was how she'd come over yesterday in some sort of obscene stretchy pants and a tight little T-shirt, neither of which covered nearly enough in his opinion.

If he were her brother, he'd have given her a lecture about how to dress in public. But he wasn't, and thank God for that, because even though he was trying not to read anything into it, something had happened last night.

Something he would never admit aloud. Something he didn't even want to admit to himself.

He'd dreamed about her.

Worse than that. He'd dreamed about them. Together. And they'd been doing—things. Hot, sweaty things.

Crap.

Zach pushed the memory away and thrust the wine toward his sister.

Amanda turned the bottle in her hand and inspected the label.

"Nice. This one didn't even come from the grocery store." She grinned, as she always did when she tried to piss him off.

The woman truly was a sadist, except this time, he wasn't going to rise to her baiting him.

He was too relaxed, on leave with nowhere to go and nothing to do.

Well, almost nothing. But the fact that the sum total of his To Do list today had consisted of buying a lampshade, rather than the usual, he was a happy man.

"I love you too, sis." Zach forced a smile, his plan

to kill Amanda with kindness—or at least maim her a little. "Want me to open that bottle for you?"

"Uh. No. That's okay."

He frowned. "Why not? You love wine."

"I do. But I don't feel like having any right now."

Zach shrugged. "Okay. Your choice." He realized they were alone in the kitchen. "Where is everybody?"

"Jasper is out back putting the chicken on the grill."

Zach nodded and waited. When she didn't continue, he prompted, "And Gabby?"

Amanda's brow shot high before her lips curved into a smile.

He realized his mistake right away. Now, because Amanda was Amanda and loved nothing more than to imagine intrigue where there was none, she was going to make a big deal out of his question.

"Why?" she asked. "Were you hoping to see her?"

"No."

Not really.

Maybe a little . . . and it had nothing to do with the dream either.

He wasn't going to admit he was a little disappointed when she didn't show up this morning. That was just because he'd come to expect her. Nothing more.

Tonight, he'd kind of wanted to tell her about his new lampshade. Prove to her even he was capable of making a good design choice . . . and even just saying that made him want to turn around, drive to the nearest range, and shoot a couple of hundred rounds before they revoked his man card.

He cleared his throat. "But I did want to ask her if

she was done and I can have my spare key back. She didn't show up today so I figured she must be finished."

"First of all it's my key to your place so when she is done she'll be returning it to me," Amanda said over her shoulder as she stood at the fridge.

"Yeah, well since you've proven you can't be trusted with a key to my place, I'm going to have to revisit my decision to give you one."

She planted the wine bottle inside the fridge and turned to stick her tongue out at him. The juvenile act had him laughing and shaking his head at the same time.

"And," Amanda continued. "Gabby didn't show up at your place today because she was doing something for her other client."

He lifted a brow. "She has more than one client?"

"Yes." Amanda scowled at him, but still reached down on one of the shelves and took out a beer.

When she held it up in offering, he nodded and walked over to take it from her. "Thanks."

"No problem." Amanda's eyes narrowed as she glanced at the digital clock on the microwave. "I actually thought she'd be back by now. I hope everything is okay."

"Why wouldn't it be?" he asked. Then he remembered the dumpster.

Was it illegal to steal trash? Had she been arrested? Or maybe she'd gotten cut and was worried about tetanus, or even rabies for that matter, depending on what was inside, so she was at the hospital.

All for a cheap decorating find. The chick really was a lunatic.

"She's in Tijuana," Amanda answered.

"Jesus, I'd forgotten about that. She actually went? And by herself?" Zach was more concerned about that than he should be considering he had no connection to Gabby other than Amanda, and she was standing here safe and sound. "What is she doing there?"

"Buying tile for the other job."

He frowned. "Why didn't she just buy it at Home Depot?"

Amanda's deep scowl was the only answer to his question. Though he couldn't figure out why. They had really nice tile there.

Buying stock tile from a nice safe, conveniently located store must have been too easy for Gabrielle Lee Interiors and More.

Not special and unique enough for the woman whose decorating concept included words like *found beauty* and *upcycling,* he supposed. And yes, he had read more of her blog before falling asleep last night.

He wouldn't do that again. It was probably what led to that dream.

"That's not illegal, is it?" Amanda asked. "Transporting tile back across the border?"

It was a hell of a time for Amanda to worry about that, after her best friend had already gone to do it.

"It might be," he answered. "If she doesn't declare what she bought at the border and pay the duty on it, and they search the vehicle and find it, maybe she could get in trouble. Or they'll just make her pay the duty before they let her across. I'm not sure. Would it be over eight hundred dollars worth?

Amanda pressed her lips together. "Probably.

She's redoing the retail space floor and half way up the walls in the front area. That's a lot of square footage. And it's hand painted tile so it's not going to be cheap. That's why she decided to drive down to get it rather than buy the imported stuff she found at the design center in San Diego."

That figured. Little miss dumpster diver did like a bargain. This time it might have gotten her into real trouble.

"What time did she leave?" he asked.

"This morning. And she said she should be back for dinner."

"Hey, bro. What's up?" Jasper slid the door to the patio closed behind him and crossed to Zach.

After a manly half-handshake, half-backslapping hug, Zach said, "Amanda's worried about Gabby."

"Why?" Jasper asked over his shoulder as he made his way to the fridge and emerged with a beer of his own.

"She's in Tijuana," Amanda answered.

"She is?" he frowned.

Jeez. Was Jasper as clueless about what was going under his own roof as he seemed? That wasn't at all encouraging.

"Remember, I'd texted you and told you to make sure Amanda didn't go to Tijuana with Gabby?" Zach asked.

Jasper's eyes widened. "You were serious? I thought it was a joke."

"No, it wasn't a joke." Zach resisted the urge to slap the man.

"She was supposed to be back by now." Amanda was starting to look really worried.

He hated to admit it, but he was getting pretty concerned himself.

"Call her," Jasper suggested, stealing a cherry tomato from the salad bowl and popping it into his mouth.

"I could do that. Wait. Can I do that? Do cell phone's work in Mexico?" She looked to Zach.

"Depends on her carrier and her plan." Zach had a feeling that a woman who got furniture in the trash and drove to Mexico to save a few bucks on tile wouldn't have a premium cell phone plan that included international roaming.

"I'm gonna try her." Amanda plunked her glass of iced tea down, pushed away from the island and reached for her cell on the counter.

Zach nodded. "Good plan."

No one was going to get to eat dinner or talk about anything else but Gabby until Amanda was certain she was okay. And actually, he'd enjoy his night a lot better once he knew that for himself too.

She might be a pain in the ass decorator, but she was *his* pain in the ass decorator.

"It's ringing," Amanda reported.

"Good." Zach took a swallow of his beer and waited.

"Hello? Gabs?" Amanda pulled the cell away from her face and checked the screen, before pressing it back against her ear. "I can't hear you. Gabby?"

After a few seconds, Amanda checked the screen again.

She looked from Zach to Jasper. "The call dropped."

"Call back," Jasper suggested.

"Okay." She nodded and tried the call again. Her eyes widened as she lowered the cell. "It went straight to voicemail."

"Look, sweetie, she probably just has really bad signal where she is." Jasper moved closer and wrapped his arm around her.

"Yeah. You're right." Amanda agreed, accepting her husband's hug.

Zach wasn't as willing to let the subject drop as he thought he'd be. "What did she say when you had her on the phone? Could you hear anything?" he asked.

"Barely. Some garbled words I couldn't understand." Amanda met his gaze. "Why? Are you worried?"

He tipped his head to one side and lifted a shoulder.

"I knew it! I'm not overreacting. This is bad." She turned to Jasper. "If *Zach* is worried, things are really bad. She could be in trouble. Kidnapped. Or arrested. Or . . . or—"

"Human trafficked," Jasper supplied when Amanda couldn't come up with any other horrible fates that might have befallen her friend.

Amanda's eyes flew wide. "Oh my God! You think?"

"Great. Thanks, Jasper. Way to calm her down." Zach rolled his eyes.

Jasper winced. "Sorry."

"We have to drive down there. We have to go find her." Amanda started for the front of the house, as if she was going to jump in the car right this minute to go find Gabby.

Zach reached out and grabbed her arm. "Oh no."

107

Amanda shot him a glare. "I'm not going to leave her down there. Alone."

"And I'm not letting you go." He leveled a no-nonsense stare on her. "I swear Amanda, I'll lock you up in handcuffs if I have to."

"You own handcuffs?" Jasper asked. "What d'you use those for?" He looked a little too interested in the answer.

Both Amanda and Zach shot Jasper a glare.

He backed up a step. "I'm going to check the chicken."

Zach lifted a brow. "Good idea."

As Jasper slunk out of the room, Amanda laid a hand on Zach's forearm. "Will you go look for her? Please?"

"Look where? Tijuana is a big place, Amanda."

"Wait. I can find out where she went." Amanda rushed to the counter and grabbed a notepad before rifling through a drawer. Finally she emerged with a pencil and started to scratch it across the pad, like a child who was too young to color and couldn't stay in the lines.

"What are you doing?" he asked.

"Gabby called the tile place from here. She wrote the address down on this pad. She took the top piece with her but I should be able to . . . yes! Look. I can see what she wrote."

Zach wandered closer and looked over her shoulder where an address revealed itself amid the scribble.

"You learn that in Girl Scouts?" he asked.

"No. Hallmark Mysteries and Movies Channel."

He shook his head and took the pad from her,

trying to decipher the letters. Between Gabby's scrawl and the fact he was trying to read through the pencil lead, it was challenging.

Zach typed what he thought the address might be into his cell's browser and it came up.

"Well?" Amanda asked, trying to see his screen.

"It is the address of a tile manufacturer in Tijuana."

Her eyes flew wide. "Oh my God. Can you go there?"

"They're going to be closed at this hour."

"But if you drive there and she broke down along the road or something, you'll find her. She put the address in her Waze App. If you do the same thing, the app will give you the same directions it gave her, right?" Amanda looked excited by her plan to solve this mystery of her missing friend.

"Yeah. I guess."

Amanda gripped his arm in both of her hands. "Please, Zach. She's got no one else here who cares about her but me. If you won't let me go, then who will help her?"

He never had been able to resist Amanda when she begged. Not when she was little and wanted him to give her his last cookie. Not when she'd come home in tears and wanted him to go threaten the boy who'd been mean to her in middle school.

And he couldn't resist her pleas now.

He glanced wistfully at the door leading to the patio where the grilled chicken he wasn't going to get to enjoy was starting to smell really good.

Knowing he was going to live to regret his words, he said, "Okay. I'll go."

She threw her arms around him. "Thank you so much."

"Don't thank me. You're going to owe me for this one."

"Anything. I promise."

"Yeah, we'll see." He let out a huff of air. "Okay. Let me get going. I'll call the minute I know anything."

"Yes. No matter what time it is. Even if it's the middle of the night."

God, he hoped he wasn't going to be up all night looking for her, but there was a good chance he would be.

This is what he got for being a nice guy.

He hauled himself into his truck and opened his contacts list on his cell.

Unlike Gabby, Zach wasn't going to go roaming around Tijuana without anyone knowing exactly where he was. Finding the contact he wanted, he hit the screen to make the call.

"Z-man. Hey, dude. What's up?" Hawk asked when he answered the phone.

"I'm on my way to Tijuana," Zach answered.

"Sounds like fun."

"Yeah, not exactly." Zach gave Hawk a quick rundown of the situation.

He needed someone besides Amanda to know where he was and what he was doing. Someone capable of doing something about it if things went sideways.

"Jesus. That's a hell of a story. You need me to come with you?" Hawk asked. "You know the buddy rule."

Zach knew the rule. Sailors were supposed to cross the border with a buddy. "Technically, I'm on leave," he said.

"Technically, you are," Hawk agreed. "But if you want the back up, I'm here. All I'm doing is packing up to head home."

A reminder Zach didn't enjoy.

"No, dude, it's fine. I'm hoping to be in and out quick," Zach began.

With any luck he'd find Gabby fast and get her back to the states with or without her load of tile.

He considered what he'd do if Gabby had been arrested by border control. That could slow things down considerably.

"But there is one thing you might be able to do for me," Zach said."

"Sure. Anything you need, you got it."

"Didn't you mention you know that SEAL who took a bullet for a senator in that shooting down in D.C.?" Zach asked.

"Zane Alexander. Yeah. I know him. I mean we're not close friends—he didn't invite me to his wedding or anything—but I know him well enough I could call him if I needed to. Why? What are you thinking?"

"I'm thinking if I have to get someone out of a Tijuana jail, you might have to make that call."

"Jesus, let's hope not. But yeah. No problem. I got you covered, Z-man."

"Thanks. Call you with the sit rep later."

"You better," Hawk warned.

"I promise." Zach disconnected the call and headed south for the border. It was going to be an interesting evening.

CHAPTER FOURTEEN

Things were going too well . . . and in Gabby's lifetime of experience, that didn't happen to her. Things didn't go smoothly. Something always went wrong.

So what was going to go wrong?

Given that she was about to drive an SUV full of Mexican tiles through Customs and Border Patrol into the US, she figured there were any number of things that could go wrong.

The nagging feeling accompanied her for miles. She couldn't even enjoy the audiobook she had playing on her Kindle, which was riding shotgun in the passenger seat.

She turned off *Protected by a SEAL* to save for later when she could enjoy it fully. She'd have to listen to the adventures of the Hollywood diva damsel in distress being rescued by the big bruiser of her Navy SEAL bodyguard later, when she wasn't afraid of being thrown into prison for trafficking tile.

She'd definitely feel better about this border crossing if it were a real SEAL sitting in the passenger seat protecting her from whatever might happen next, rather than her eReader.

Since she only knew one big scary SEAL, and yesterday she hadn't been brave enough to ask him to go with her on this trip, she was flying solo. Or rather driving, if she could even call this driving as she slowed for the ever increasing traffic heading toward the US border.

She'd read online in her Tijuana research that there could be a two-hour wait at the border. Even worse on weekends. She'd chosen to come mid-week, hoping for less of a delay getting back into the States.

But as the US border grew nearer, according to the GPS app on her cell, she was starting to hope for a delay because she wasn't ready for this.

She was shaking.

The border guard would take one look at her and give her a cavity search, because she definitely looked suspicious.

She felt suspicious, even if she had dotted all the I's and crossed all the T's. She had her invoice ready to show at the border. She had cash in US Dollars and Pesos, as well as a credit card and her checkbook to pay any duty she might owe on the tile. She should be all set.

Wait, where was that invoice? She panicked and looked down at the seat next to her.

It wasn't there.

Glancing up she remembered she'd stuck it in the visor, but then the sun had been in her eyes and she'd lowered that so she'd stuck the invoice somewhere else.

One hand on the steering wheel, she glanced at the passenger seat visor, just as her cell phone started to ring in its dashboard holder.

This was the second time Amanda had called since she'd been on the way home.

The first time had been a while ago. She'd answered but the signal had been such crap the call dropped almost immediately.

Amanda was probably worried about her. Gabby needed to at least try to answer.

She reached to touch the screen icon to connect the call, then she had to visually locate and touch the icon to put it on speaker phone.

"Hello!" She yelled at the cell, finally looking up at the highway in front of her just in time.

She hit the brake pedal hard and barely avoided slamming into the car that had zipped into her lane and cut her off.

The sudden stop rocked the SUV hard enough she flew forward toward the steering wheel until the seat belt cutting across her held her back.

The cell phone went flying out of its already precarious perch in the two-dollar vent holder she'd been meaning to replace with a better one.

And the tile—good God, the tile. The thousands of dollars worth of tile, in cardboard boxes with no padding or protection, all slid forward behind her, the boxes crashing against the back of the driver and the passenger seats.

Her Kindle took a header for the floor, but worse than that, she swore she heard the subtle crack of ceramic behind her.

She didn't know what to rescue first.

The tile—her precious cargo—was uppermost in her mind. But, there was also her cell phone, which might or might not still have a call connected to

Amanda active.

However, that was somewhere out of sight on the floorboards. Possibly under the pedals beneath her feet, which could not be good.

What if she hit the accelerator or the brake and the phone was wedged under there? She leaned down and tried to look as the traffic streamed around her stopped car, horns blaring as her nerves reached the breaking point.

She couldn't see anything under there without a light, which was on her cell phone, lost on the dark floor.

It was clear she had to pull over—across three lanes of traffic to get to the closest shoulder. She'd just have to risk it.

Slowly, agonizingly slowly, amid enough chaos and road rage to rattle even the Pope's nerves, she made her way over to the side of the road.

She stopped the vehicle far enough over she'd be safe from the crazy drivers and threw it into *park*. Only then did she feel like she could breathe freely again. But there was so much more to do, and she still had to get across the border.

This plan was looking less and less wise as the day progressed.

Nothing she could do about it now.

She unhooked the seatbelt and opened the driver's side door. First things first. Standing next to the car, she bent down and tried to see the floor. No luck.

Blindly, she reached down and ran her hands around under the seat.

Finally her fingers hit something smooth. She grabbed the cell and pulled it out.

The screen wasn't broken. That was one stroke of

good luck. But it had powered itself off. Not a great sign, but it might be all right.

She hit the power button and waited . . . Finally the little white apple appeared in the center of the screen and she let out the breath she'd been holding.

While the cell powered itself back on, she shoved it into her back pocket.

Next on her list of priorities was the tile.

She probably should have been more concerned about the thousands of dollars of tile rather than her cell phone in the first place. She'd have to deal with her tech addiction later when she was back on US soil, which she might never leave again after this experience.

Pulled over on the side of the road wasn't the safest place to be but she needed to calm down a bit from the near crash, and she'd feel a lot better once she'd checked on her cargo.

She spotted the invoice, the cause of all of this mess to begin with. Reaching in, she grabbed it, vowing to keep it in sight until she crossed that border.

The damn thing was written in Spanish but the number of cases was listed in numerals so that she could understand.

Twenty boxes, tight packed in the back of her SUV, just fit with the back seats flipped down.

It was enough to do the shop with a few—very few—to spare in case of breakage. She hoped she hadn't blown through the extras already by slamming on the brakes.

She had to check. Better to know now.

Slipping her fingers into the crevice in the cardboard, she tugged. It didn't budge. The flaps were glued shut. She pulled harder and slipped, tearing off the tip of one nail in the process.

"Ow."

That had hurt. She wasn't the type who could maintain a manicure since she worked with her hands so often, so she didn't bother getting her nails done. But perfectly polished or not, she still liked to keep her nails on her fingers.

She inspected the damage, wondering if she even had a nail file in her bag or if she'd have to drive all the way home with the ragged nail.

"Need a little help?" The sound of the man's voice directly behind her had her jumping.

Hand pressed to her chest, she spun—and let out a breath of relief. "Zach."

He folded his arms across his chest, his gaze resting on her. "Gabby."

As her heart continued to pound from the scare, she asked, "What are you doing here?"

"I could ask you the same thing."

"I came to get tile."

"Yes, so Amanda said. But seriously, driving down here alone—what were you thinking?"

"That I could save the client money." And make a bit of profit for herself by adding a ten percent fee while still keeping the cost well below what it would have been locally. "But what are you doing here? Were you down here for the day?"

He looked at her like she was a lunatic. "No. I came to find you."

Really?

She frowned. "How did you even know I was here?"

"Amanda. She's flipping out because you said

you'd be home by dinner."

"Oh. Yeah. The trip took a little longer than I expected. First I was hungry and I'd read online that the place that invented the Caesar salad is down here and still in business so I had to go there. Then I stopped in a few shops. Then I had to get to the tile place and wait for them to load my car . . ." She let the sentence trail off as he shook his head.

How could he relay so much judgment in one little headshake?

Finally he let out a breath. "Are you done with all your sightseeing and shopping? Can we get you back across the border now?"

"Yes. I just have to check the tile."

"Here? Now? Couldn't you have done that at the tile place?"

"Yes," and she should have but she didn't. It didn't matter anyway because that was before the near crash. "But I just had to slam on my brakes and everything shifted pretty hard and I'm afraid some broke."

"So you decided to check on the side of the highway?" His chin dropped as he shook his head, clearly unhappy with her decision.

"If I need to go back and buy more I'd rather know now." She defended her action with logic even Zach shouldn't be able to dispute.

"They won't still be open now, but fine. We'll check the load and then get back on the road. Okay?"

"Yes." But now that she agreed she realized the logistical issues of having to unload twenty cases, check them all, then load them back inside again.

They'd be lucky if they didn't attract some sort of highway patrol and that was the last thing she wanted.

Maybe they could check just the front row of boxes.

Zach was already tearing into the cardboard, seemingly unperturbed. He had no problem tearing the two sides apart without causing himself bodily injury.

He spread the cardboard flaps wide and glanced at her.

"The top ones are perfect. See?" he asked as he took one step to the side so she could get a view inside the box past him.

"Yes. Thank you."

He nodded, then hoisted up the heavy box and gave it a bit of a shake. "I don't hear any movement. I don't think the underneath ones are broken. Do you still want to check them?" he asked.

She cringed, afraid to tell him the truth.

Yes, she did want to check them and in fact should have while they were being loaded, but he was already being so nice helping her, how could she ask him to inspect all the tile piece by piece?

She hesitated long enough after his question, he didn't wait for her answer. He put the box back down with a sigh and said, "Yes, you do want to check them all. Okay."

"Maybe just all of them in one—or maybe two—boxes."

He ignored her and started to take the tiles out, stacking them neatly on top of the sealed box next to him. He got almost all of the way down to the bottom and pulled out a piece of cardboard, then went still.

"Fuck." He started loading the tile back inside the box, fast. "Gabby, get in the car."

"Why? What's wrong?"

He finished reloading the box and slammed the

cargo hatch. When he turned to look at her, his expression was more glacial than usual.

Jaw tight, nostrils flaring, he said, "Get in the car."

"Tell me what's wrong."

He hooked her arm in an iron grip, leading her around the car to the driver's side. "Get in the car, Gabby. Now."

"I don't—"

"There are drugs in those boxes."

"What?" Her eyes flew wide. "I didn't—"

"I know you didn't, but your bargain tile dealer did. Follow me."

"Where?"

"I'll figure that out when I get there. Just stay on my tail." He turned toward his truck and squinted across the highway. "How long has that van been parked there?"

"What van?" she asked, frowning in the direction he'd been looking against the glare of the sun that was just dipped halfway below the horizon.

He sent her a wide-eyed stare. "Never mind. Hop over to the passenger seat. I'm driving."

"But what about your truck?"

He aimed his own key fob at his truck and clicked to lock the doors then slid into the driver's seat. "It's going to have to stay there for now. I'm more worried about getting us and your load of drugs out of here before whoever owns it figures out we know and they decide to come get it."

She buckled in and held on tight to the armrest as he pulled out into traffic. Zach somehow managed to zip between the cars and across all of the lanes before steering them off the road and across the grass median.

As the vehicle bottomed out in a low spot she heard the boxes in back bouncing. She hissed in a breath and he shot her a glare.

"Stop. I'll buy you new fucking tile if it breaks, but I'm not getting killed over that shit back there."

It wasn't shit. It was gorgeous hand painted tiles—made as a cover to traffic drugs into the US apparently. And they'd seen her as the perfect mule.

Jeez. This was the stuff of crime shows on TV, not her life. But it somehow had become her life, and now Zach's too because of her.

She kept all thoughts to herself. Probably the only smart thing she'd done since deciding to buy the damn tile in the first place.

Instead, she prayed they'd get out of this thing alive.

CHAPTER FIFTEEN

It took a bit of skill and a lot of law breaking, but Zach shook the van that might or might not have been tailing them. He still wasn't sure which.

There was a good chance if they'd put drugs in her car, they'd also put a tracker so they could retrieve their stash once she'd gotten it across the border. But that didn't mean they wouldn't keep eyes on her to make sure she didn't unload those boxes somewhere en route.

All of his maneuvering put them in downtown Tijuana where he figured they could hide amid the tourists while they figured things out. But it also put him miles away from where he'd left his truck.

Man, did they have a lot to figure out, like what to do with the drugs in the back and what to do about the drug dealers who would no doubt be looking to get their stash back.

And last but not least, how to get his vehicle someplace safe before it was towed or stolen. He wasn't all that into material things but dammit, he loved that truck.

Time to call in a favor.

Reaching for his cell, he struggled to get it out of his pocket while slowly cruising the streets and watching for the reappearance of the tail.

"Who are you calling," Gabby asked. "And you're not supposed to hold the phone while you drive."

He cocked up a brow as he punched the screen to connect with Hawk and sent Gabby a glare. "And you're not supposed to transport drugs across the border so . . ."

She pouted and mumbled, "I was just saying that I have a dashboard holder if you want to use it."

He glanced at the dash and saw none.

"It fell on the floor," she continued when she noticed his glance.

Zach let out a breath as Hawk answered the call.

"Z-man, please tell me no one is in prison."

"Not yet." Unfortunately, it was still a very real possibility one or both of them could end up there. "Look I need a huge favor from you. And you're going to have to get one of the other guys to come with you."

Zach realized that might be easier said than done. Compass and Dutch had headed off to Alaska, of all places, the day after they'd all met at the bar. And Rocket had left for Vegas directly from McP's the night they were all there.

"Sure. What is it?"

"I need you to drive across the border and one of you has to drive my truck back. It's parked on the Mexican side on the shoulder of the North bound lane of Highway 1, two miles from the San Ysidro border crossing. There's a hide-a-key near the driver's side rear wheel well.

"Um, okay. I can do that. Is everything okay?" he asked.

That's what Zach loved about his teammates. When push came to shove they'd do anything for him, no questions asked. Even when he was asking them to do something this crazy, if he offered no other explanation than he needed them to do it, they would.

But in this case, he did need to tell Hawk what was happening because this pile of shit Gabby had gotten herself into might be more than Zach could handle on his own.

Hawk had asked if everything was okay. Not quite.

"Well, it seems Gabby's tile dealer is dealing more than tile. I was checking her load and found something."

"Oh, shit. How much?" Hawk asked, guessing the content of those boxes correctly.

"I don't know. She's got about two dozen boxes in the car and I only checked one." One had been enough for him to know they had to get the hell off the side of the road where a patrol could stop by any moment.

Hawk let out a long low whistle. "What are you going to do?"

Zach laughed. "Good question. Got any answers?"

"Let me call Alexander. He has a fuck-ton of contacts in DC. He'll know what to do. This could be a good thing."

Zach blew out a snort. "Oh really. How's that?"

"The authorities might be able to use Gabby's little mishap to shut down a major drug runner. Who knows?"

Who knew, indeed?

"All right. Make the call," Zach agreed.

"Expect a call back from either me or him shortly," Hawk continued.

"Thanks, Hawk."

"You got it, bro."

Zach disconnected the call and blew out a long slow breath before he glanced at Gabby. She looked shaken but to her credit she was holding it mostly together.

Thank God, because he didn't need hysteria on top of everything else.

"You all right?" he asked.

"Yeah."

He lifted a brow. "Really?"

"Yes. You're here."

The comment took him by surprise. It was a few seconds before he could absorb all the ramifications of Gabby's blind trust in him to save her in this pretty dire situation.

Finally, he swallowed. "It's gonna work out."

She dipped her head, her gaze holding his. "I know. I trust you."

Again her blind trust struck him like a physical blow.

On the team they depended on one another, but they were also equally skilled, highly trained, combat hardened operators.

It was rare he was put in this position, protecting someone so completely innocent and—he hated to say it—helpless.

She might be a strong woman—at least she sure as hell was strong willed—but none of that mattered against a Mexican drug cartel or the authorities, both who would be looking to grab her because of what was in her vehicle.

But Gabby didn't need the reminder of that truth and he wasn't about to risk pushing her into the breakdown they'd avoided so far.

He needed a distraction and found one out the side window. "Look. There's your Caesar Salad place."

She glanced out the window and then back. "Yeah. Are you hungry?" she asked.

He was starving, but now wasn't the time to stop for a meal.

"Because I have some granola bars if you want." She reached into the console and emerged with one, handing it to him. "I have water bottles too, in an insulated bag by my feet."

Smiling, he reached for the bar she offered. "Thanks. This is good."

Nope. Not helpless, but certainly good at stepping in shit, this one.

His cell rang and an unfamiliar number flashed across the screen. He answered the call, "Hello?"

"Master Chief Browne?"

"Yes." Shit, he really hoped he wasn't about to get recalled from leave for a mission. This was the worst possible timing.

Please don't be command and please don't ask where I am.

"Zane Alexander here. Jace Hawkins called and said you're in a bit of a situation."

"Yes, sir. That's right."

"You can call me Zane, Master Chief."

"And you can call me Zach."

"All right, Zach. I need a sit rep, starting with your current location."

The no nonsense orders coming from the former

SEAL put Zach right back into his comfort zone. This was like any other mission—almost. He might have started this on his own and without backup, but it felt like that was rapidly changing. He had a team behind him again and in his current situation that was incredibly comforting.

Zach hit to put the call on speaker phone and navigated on his screen. "I'm texting you our exact GPS location now."

"Got it," Zane said. "Now tell me about these drugs and this . . . tile is it?"

"Yes." He shot Gabby a look.

It sounded as if her exploits had managed to baffle the combat hardened SEAL on the phone, who'd no doubt seen and heard a lot during his career in and out of the service. Had to admire that skill in a woman.

Zach told the story, everything he knew, including the make, model and year of Gabby's vehicle.

When he didn't have all the facts, Gabby filled them in. Such as her license plate number, who had loaded the car, and who had taken her payment for the tile.

She did well, telling the story concisely and with detail.

Zane blew out a breath. "That's one hell of a situation you two are in. But I've got someone listening in who I think can help."

Well, shit. Someone was listening in? That would have been nice to know in advance. This whole thing had better not blow back on Gabby.

But what else could he have done but call in backup? Dumping the drugs wasn't an option, even if they could find any tracking devices hidden on the car. Not when the dealer had all of Gabby's information and could easily track her down.

He had to trust Zane and his D.C. contacts to not screw them. Trusting Zane, a former SEAL, was easy. Wrapping his head around trusting Washington bureaucrats was another thing altogether.

"Zach, this is Silas Branson with the DHS."

Holy shit. Now the Department of Homeland Security was involved? Zach was starting to second-guess his decision to involve Zane Alexander, if this was the result.

"Can you and Miss Lee hear me?" Branson asked.

"Yes, sir."

"No need for the sir. I left the SEALs and being Lieutenant Commander a few years ago. I'm just Silas now."

Jesus, it seemed you couldn't throw a rock nowadays without hitting a SEAL.

Okay, at least the DHS dude was a team guy—an officer, but a SEAL nonetheless. In this case, it felt like a good thing that it was a fellow frogman involved with saving them.

"Yes, sir—Silas," Zach corrected himself.

"First I need you to know I'm assembling a team and you and Miss Lee will be covered throughout the entire operation."

There was a team and an operation now? Zach shot Gabby a glance. She was starting to look less calm.

"All right," Zach said, wondering how this team had been assembled so quickly given Silas was, as far as he knew, across the country in D.C. with Zane.

The man had a long reach.

"We're going to need you to cross the border back

into the US."

"With the—um—boxes intact?" Zach asked, not relishing the idea of driving through border control with a bunch of drugs.

Maybe that was the plan? Border control would make a big show of seizing the drugs, which would hopefully be witnessed by the dealers. They'd know Gabby was no longer in possession and she'd be off the hook.

"We've arranged it so you'll be cleared through," Silas said.

And there went that theory.

"And then what?" Zach asked.

"Then you go home."

"With the drugs?" he asked.

"Yes."

Zach mouthed a silent curse.

"What?" Gabby whispered.

Eyes narrowed in anger, he answered, "They're using you as bait."

"That's correct," Silas confirmed matter-of-factly, as if it were okay.

It wasn't okay in Zach's book. "I'm not onboard with this plan."

"Miss Lee's house will be under surveillance the entire time."

"Yeah, see that's part of the problem. Miss Lee is currently living with my sister in her home with her husband and there's no fucking way I'm letting you put my family on some drug cartel's radar."

There was a moment of silence on the other end of the phone and Zach didn't know if they'd muted the call to discuss him or if they were just speechless that he wasn't going to roll over and do as ordered.

This was not a Navy mission and he didn't have to be a good little SEAL.

"A hotel is an option," Zane suggested.

"I'd rather someplace with less civilian traffic, if possible. A quiet neighborhood," Silas said.

For less collateral damage when things went south, no doubt. Zach shook his head at the thought.

"We'll never be able to locate a rental house in that area on an hour's notice," Zane said.

Rental. At Zanc's words, an idea struck Zach and he liked it.

Compass's old place.

Jace Hawkins wasn't the only one leaving the team. Rio North was already moved out of his place.

The landlord wouldn't be thrilled to know Zach and the DHS were about to use the vacant apartment as bait for a drug runner's thugs, but what he didn't know wouldn't hurt him.

The man rented to sailors. No doubt he had good homeowner's insurance.

"I might know of a place," Zach said.

"Go on," Silas prompted.

"My teammate recently put in his papers. His rental is empty but he's paid up until the first of next month." Zach didn't have a key but that wasn't a problem. A SEAL could pick a lock quicker than a thief any day.

"Address?" Silas asked.

Zach rattled off the address of the house where he'd gotten drunk—and slept it off—played cards and watched almost every big game for the past five years or so.

Compass always complained about his apartment, but it was perfect as far as the team was concerned. It was conveniently located and Compass was a good host.

He'd been the first among them to invest in an insanely large flat screen television. That made his place party central. And tonight Compass's empty apartment, and his parking spot in the garage, would serve Zach's purposes perfectly.

"Great," Silas said. "We'll send the team to set up surveillance in the neighborhood. You drive there, leave the boxes in the car and go inside. Pretend everything is normal. We'll handle the rest."

"What if they don't come for the drugs tonight?" Zach asked.

"They will. They're not going to want to risk them being discovered."

"Okay. We're heading to the border now." He hesitated. "You sure you got that border crossing covered? I'm in no mood for a cavity search."

He also wasn't in the mood to spend the night in a Mexican jail and he'd rather Gabby never have that experience either.

Silas laughed. "You're good. I've already been on the phone with the commissioner of Customs and Border Protection.

Satisfied with that answer, Zach said, "All right. I'm hanging up and heading there now."

"We're with you all the way," Silas said one more time.

Zach only hoped it was the truth. He disconnected the call and glanced at Gabby. "You ready for this?"

She shook her head. "No."

"We're gonna be fine."

"Will you stay with me? In your friend's house?" she asked.

"Yeah. I'm with you for as long as it takes." He reached out and squeezed her hand before realizing it felt too—intimate? He hated the word but it fit.

Intimate and nice. It felt good to hold Gabby's hand—and that's why he let it drop.

"What about my tile?" she asked. "You don't think they're going to seize it as evidence, do you?"

He shot her a glance. "They might."

Her eyes widened. "Well they can't. I need it for the job. I don't get final payment until I finish."

He let out a short laugh. "One day you're really going to have to consider your priorities."

She screwed up her mouth. "You're not the first one to tell me that."

He let out a snort. "Not surprised."

"Zach," she said.

"Yeah?" He glanced at her, one hand resting on the gearshift in the center console.

"I'm kind of starving. Maybe once we're across we can stop. I know this isn't a good time—"

"No. It's the perfect time." He was starving too. That crunchy bar Gabby had given him had been like chewing on sawdust covered in chocolate. And he enjoyed a woman who wasn't afraid to eat in front of a man.

Fuck it.

If they were going to be the DHS's bait for a drug runner the minute they crossed the border, then he was all for delaying that event for an hour or so.

"They have anything other than salad at that Caesar's place?" He tipped his chin toward the restaurant just a little way down the street.

Zach needed time to think, weigh what was happening, plan a contingency. A quick half hour meal would provide that, and get some food in both their stomachs.

He could follow orders but he could also think on his feet. Blindly following his command's orders was one thing, but Zane and Silas were strangers to him—civilian strangers now by their own admittance.

"Yes." She nodded in answer to his question. "Everything on the menu looked really good."

It had been a while since he'd enjoyed a night in Tijuana. Tonight with Gabby wouldn't be anything like those nights on liberty with the team, but it would do.

He pulled the key out of the ignition and shot her a smile. "Let's go. And we can call Amanda from the restaurant. She's worried about you."

Gabby lifted a brow. "And us telling her about my trunk filled with drugs will make her feel better?"

Hand on the door handle he shot her a glance. "How about we leave that part out?" he suggested.

"Do you know your sister?" she asked, the question ripe with sarcasm.

She was right. His sister should have gone into the legal profession, or maybe law enforcement. She could conduct an investigation and fire off the questions better than any prosecutor.

He drew in a breath. "Okay, maybe we text her instead, then turn off your phone."

"Much better plan." She nodded then paused, not moving to get out of the SUV. "Zach. In case we don't get out of this and we end up dead or in prison, I just wanted to say thank you."

He halted. She might think she was joking when she mentioned death and prison, but the possibility wasn't too far from the truth.

"Don't thank me yet."

CHAPTER SIXTEEN

Zach's gaze remained trained on the line of cars in front of them.

Gabby was happy to be in traffic. In fact, she'd be happy if they didn't move at all for a good long while.

The closer they crept toward the border crossing, the tighter her chest felt. It was as if her ribs were slowly closing in on her organs. She couldn't draw in enough breath. Even her heart felt like it labored just to beat.

"Breathe," Zach said softly.

The deep sexy timbre of his voice would have had her breathless *if* she could get air into her lungs.

She tried sucking in a breath and it came in a stuttered series of starts and stops.

"Jesus, Gabby. Please don't hyperventilate. I've got enough to worry about at the moment."

"I'm sorry." Her voice broke on the final word.

He finally glanced in her direction. "We're gonna be okay."

Biting her lip, she nodded.

He muttered a curse and reached out one hand,

grasping her shoulder with his strong grip. She forced herself to fight the tears hovering just below the surface and look at him.

"Just hang on a little bit longer. Can you do that for me?" he asked.

Why now, of all times, did he have to be sweet?

How many nights had she dreamed of this man's hands on her as he spoke soft words of encouragement to her? And now it was happening but only because she was probably going to end up in a Tijuana jail for drug smuggling—after they confiscated her tile and insured she never got paid for her job.

"I'll try," she whispered.

"That's my girl."

His girl. She swallowed hard. Maybe, just maybe, if they made it through this night—

Then what? What was she hoping for?

She knew what she wanted, and always had, and that was Zach's lips on hers. His hands all over her body.

She tried and failed to yank her mind off the image of him in bed, naked, braced over her as she spread her legs for him.

Since that little fantasy becoming reality was not going to happen, she'd settle for them just having a good relationship. One where she could be at Amanda's house and Zach wouldn't glare at her.

Him picking up his cell and punching in a text brought her out of her own head and back to the horror of her reality. "Who are you texting?"

"Alexander. Telling him and Branson we're about to cross the border." He glanced in her direction. "And telling them which lane we're in. Figure it can't hurt to be specific."

Oh God. The border guard was going to drag her out of the car and lock her up forever.

She glanced behind her at the twenty cardboard boxes they had no hope of hiding, even in the dark of night, because the border crossing was lit up like the Vegas strip.

They were going to be strip searched and then thrown in a Tijuana jail for sure.

"Here we go." His voice didn't relay any of her panic.

She whipped her gaze to look forward and saw there was only one car in front of them now, and it was moving forward to allow them to pull into its place in front of the guard.

It was their turn.

"Oh my God." She felt lightheaded and reached for the armrest.

"Relax and give me your ID." His slow measured words were too calm.

Why wasn't he worried? The man wasn't human.

"My ID. My ID. Oh my God. Where did I put it?"

"You stuck it in the visor along with the invoice. Remember?"

"Yes. Phew." She reached for the visor and yanked it down, sending everything flying.

In the dark of the car, she started to panic as she felt around on the floor by her feet.

She grabbed the invoice easily since it was so large and shoved it under her butt on the seat where it would stay put. Then she went back in, looking for her license.

Meanwhile, Zach had rolled down the window and already handed his ID to the guard. "She's just looking for hers."

His words sent a renewed sense of panic through her and she leaned forward farther, nearly choking herself with the seatbelt still buckled.

She felt blindly by her feet, cursing the dark.

Finally her hand struck on the smooth small rectangle of her license. She grabbed it, popped upright, and thrust it toward Zach. "Here"

"Here you go." He smiled at the guard. The guard ducked down and peered at her, comparing the photo on the ID.

The guard handed both pieces of identification back to Zach and nodded. "Have a good night."

"Thank you."

"Don't you need the invoice—"

"Shh," Zach hissed as he hit the gas while closing the window. "Don't offer up what they didn't ask for."

"But they didn't ask us for anything other than ID. Or look in the car." She watched behind them in the mirror, half expecting to see flashing lights and hear sirens because they'd realized their mistake.

"You're going to complain we got through too easily?" He shook his head. "Branson said he'd arranged for us to get across the border without any trouble. I'm just glad he's a man of his word."

"Me too." She blew out a breath and asked, "So that's it?"

"No. That's definitely not it. This is far from over. Now we get to be bait."

She'd been so paralyzed with fear over crossing the border, she'd kind of forgotten about that other part.

At least she'd pushed it out of her mind. Self preservation.

There was only so much trauma her psyche could handle at once. Tonight she'd reached the limit . . . more than once. And she'd dragged Zach into it with her.

She glanced at him as he drove. "You don't have to stay with me. I know I asked you to, but you can go. I'll be fine."

He turned and frowned. "Stop. I'm in this to the end."

Her heart warmed. "Thank you."

"You're welcome."

"How far to your friend's house?" she asked.

"Not far."

By the time Zach had them speeding North on Interstate 5, she'd circled around the same problem so much her head was spinning.

Now that they were back on US soil, she could afford to think about her other problems—namely, saving her job.

"I can't let them take this tile," she said as the knowledge of exactly how screwed she would be on the shop job without it hit her. The tile was the cornerstone of the whole design plan.

One hand draped casually on the steering wheel, he glanced at her. "We don't have much choice."

"Why not?" she asked. "Why can't we just hide somewhere out of sight and empty the tile out of all those boxes? Just the tile, not the drugs, of course. Then we put the empty boxes back in the car with the drugs still inside for the drug dealers to come steal back."

"They're gonna notice—" The ringing of his cell interrupted Zach. Drawing in a breath, he swiped the screen and pressed the phone to his ear. "Hey."

She wished he'd put it on speakerphone. He didn't, so she leaned closer and tried to hear.

Zach listened to whoever was on the call. Finally, he said, "Bring the truck to Compass's place . . . and Hawk, you got any extra cardboard boxes from your move?"

It must be the friend who'd gone to retrieve Zach's truck. She'd been so worried about herself, she'd almost forgotten he'd abandoned his vehicle along the side of the road in Mexico, all to help her.

But wait—what was that he'd said about cardboard boxes?

"Good. Bring those too. I'll see you there." Zach disconnected the call.

She waited, heart pounding, but he didn't explain as he slowed and steered off the exit. She read the passing signs for Coronado as they headed for what she could only assume was his buddy's abandoned apartment.

Maybe if the rent was cheap enough she could move in there since she was still homeless. But it would have to be really cheap since the flood of new jobs she'd been counting on hadn't happened yet.

Finally, Zach slowed the vehicle and swung into a driveway. His truck was already parked at the curb, along with another black pick-up with two guys leaning against it.

Zach threw her car in *park* and said, "Wait here while I open the garage door."

He reached to open his door when she grabbed for his forearm. "Wait. What are we doing?"

Glancing back at her, he said, "Saving your damn tile."

140

CHAPTER SEVENTEEN

"You sure you guys are okay with dropping this stuff off?" Zach asked, slamming the tailgate on Hawk's four-wheel-drive king cab.

"Yeah, no problem. And given this unique set of circumstances, better us than you two," Hawk said, tipping his head toward Gabby, who looked reluctant to part with the precious tile stashed in the moving boxes in the bed of Hawk's pick-up.

Zach had to agree with Hawk. He was at a bit of a disadvantage in this situation. He had no weapon and he had Gabby.

Meanwhile, Hawk was armed and had another SEAL with him. Hawk had grabbed Lopez, the lucky, or rather unlucky guy, from McP's to help after Zach's SOS call from across the border.

"You have the code to get into the back door of the shop?" Gabby asked.

"Yes, Gabby." Hawk smiled indulgently.

She eyed the boxes then looked up at the tall man and cringed. "Please drive slow so it doesn't break."

"I promise," Hawk made the shape of an X over

his heart while the SEAL Zach knew by name but not well stood back and looked amused.

"You can just put it right inside the back door—"

"Gabby," Zach interrupted. "The tile will be fine. They've got to get going."

It was almost midnight and he was well aware they were on a ticking clock. It was only a matter of time before the owners of the drugs still inside the cardboard boxes in Gabby's trunk would arrive.

He'd grabbed her arm to steer her away when she planted her feet in the ground and said to Hawk, "Thank you so much for all your help tonight."

"Anytime." Lopez smiled, looking a bit too flirty and interested in Gabby for Zach's taste.

Hawk grinned. "It's what we do. We help each other."

Ready to be out of there, Zach tipped his chin towards the two men. "Yeah, thanks, both of you. And Hawk, call me before you leave town."

"Oh, I'll be calling you in the morning. You know, for a sit rep." With a grin, Hawk turned toward his truck.

Zach knew the kind of report Hawk wanted in the morning had more to do with the night he was about to spend in Gabby's company, and less to do with drug runners.

Not that there was all that much night left. But what there was left, he intended to spend in his own damn bed. Not on the bare mattress in Compass's rental, whether Silas and the DHS liked it or not.

While Gabby had spent the drive back worrying about tile, Zach had done a bit of thinking himself.

Whoever had put those drugs in Gabby's boxes weren't after her tile. They'd be coming to retrieve their stash, which they'd discovered was hidden beneath the false cardboard bottom of every single one of her tile boxes. All twenty of them.

So why shouldn't she save her tile? And why should they stay as human bait?

If there was a tracker, it would be in the boxes still in the car, or on the car itself. They'd come and find the car, and the boxes, and their drugs, but they weren't going to find Gabby.

He'd leave her car there but he was taking her in his truck back to his place. And Zach didn't give a shit if that wasn't what DHS had told them to do.

Compass always complained about his landlord and his crap apartment, but the one good thing it had was a big garage. That feature had come in particularly useful tonight.

It had taken some maneuvering but they'd managed to empty the tile out of Gabby's car while out of sight inside the garage. They'd pulled her car out and drove Hawk's truck in, where they loaded the tile into the moving boxes in the back—all behind the privacy of the closed door.

Now, Zach heaved up the big garage door so Hawk could drive out.

When Hawk and Lopez and the prized tile was gone, he pulled Gabby's car back in and left the door open so the bad guys had no trouble locating their booty. The point was to make it easy for the them to get in and take the stash so the good guys could catch them.

It was a good plan. At least he liked it. Zane and Silas might have another opinion.

Was the DHS team already there set up in the neighbors' houses or maybe in a parked car somewhere nearby?

"Come on. Time to go." He handed Gabby up into the passenger seat of his truck—the truck he was most grateful to see again and in perfect condition after leaving it along the side of the road in Mexico.

He drove away half expecting to get a phone call from Silas reprimanding him for leaving. But he didn't.

Zach made it all the way to his own house without a peep from anyone. That was a good sign, he hoped.

He pulled into the driveway and cut the engine, turning to glance at Gabby. She'd been silent the whole drive over.

"You okay?"

"Just trying to take it all in."

He laughed. "Good luck with that. It's a lot."

"Yeah."

"You want me to take you to Amanda's?" It was a half hour drive and past midnight, hella inconvenient, but he'd do it.

Why, he didn't know. He must be getting soft in his old age.

"No. It's late. I don't want to wake her. And then she'll want to hear everything and I'll never get any sleep." She glanced up at him. "You don't mind me being here, do you? I can go back to Amanda's—"

"Gabby, it's fine. I invited you." He smiled. "Besides, you haven't seen my new lampshade yet."

"Well, I don't want to miss that." She laughed.

"Come on. I've got a guest room all set up for guests for some reason." He sent her a sideways glance as he slid out of the driver's seat.

"This is the reason," she said loud enough for him to hear as she got out of the passenger door.

"Everyone should have a room for unexpected guests—who are on the run from Mexican drug lords."

He laughed as he walked around the truck to her side. He reached out and braced a hand on the back of her neck, beneath her long fall of hair. "You did good tonight."

"Did I?" she asked, sounding surprised.

"You did," he said, as they walked toward the door. And he meant it.

He'd been braced for hysterics. He didn't get them. Her obsession with the damn tile had been the only real issue tonight.

Yup. Tonight could have been worse. So much worse.

He drew in a breath as he put the key in the door. "I could use a drink."

"You and me both."

"Lucky for you I'm well stocked in that department."

"At this point I'd drink rubbing alcohol, but that's good to hear."

He grinned. She was funny and clever and . . . quirky.

That was a good word for all of the things that were uniquely Gabby. He hadn't appreciated all that about her before. He wasn't sure how he felt about the fact that he appreciated it now.

Inside, she pulled her cell out of her pocket and glanced at it. "Dead."

"Lucky for you I have a charging station. Come with me, madam." With a sweep of his hand, he ushered her to the box and opened the lid. "As you see we have one of every kind of cord for all of your device charging needs."

"I knew that multi-cord would come in handy." She smiled looking genuinely thrilled he was using her contraption.

"And you were right," he had to admit.

She plugged in her cell and turned to him. "Thank you for tonight. I want you to know how hugely grateful I am for your help. And your friends who came. And Amanda for letting me stay there. I don't know what I'll do without you all—"

Her voice cracked on the last word.

Zach frowned as he saw the tears in her eyes.

"Whoa. Wait. What's going on? Everything's fine. There's no need to cry now." He reached out and brushed one tear from her cheek. "We're safe."

She shook her head. "It's not just tonight. It's that on the drive, I did some math."

Math?

"You did what?" he asked.

"I ran some numbers in my head and even after I finish the shop and get paid, I'm not earning enough to stay here. Not now that I lost my apartment. I guess I'd been hoping with a few completed projects in my portfolio, the jobs would come rolling in." She drew in a breath and straightened her spine. "But they haven't and now it's time to face facts. I can't keep living with Amanda forever. I'm going to have to go home to my parents' house and move in with them like a twenty-nine year old loser."

She bit her lip and visibly fought the tears.

"Come here." Zach reached out and pulled her to him wrapping his arms around her. "You're not a loser. Starting a business is hard. And this isn't exactly an affordable area to live in."

She nodded against his chest as he spoke, her arms wrapped around his waist.

"I'm sure you'll figure something out. You're very innovative. I mean who else could have furnished my whole house with trash?" Smiling he smoothed a hand down the silky length of her hair.

She drew in a deep breath and pulled back just far enough she could look up at him. "Thanks for the pep talk."

"Anytime." He brushed a stray hair off her face with the back of his hand, but found his fingers lingering there against the soft warmth of her cheek.

He leaned in, or maybe she did. He wasn't sure. But somehow their faces ended up just a breath apart. Their lips so close it seemed natural that he should close the distance and press his against hers.

He'd known her for most of his adult life. And tonight, they'd traveled to hell and back—or at least to Tijuana and back with a load of drugs.

They'd shared a meal together. She and he had both been there for more than a decade's worth of monumental moments in his sister's life.

And that was why he shouldn't angle his head and thrust his tongue between her lips, even if he wanted to. Why he shouldn't thrust inside the wet heat of her mouth until his cock was so hard it pounded against his zipper to be let out.

Nope. Shouldn't do any of that.

Even so, he moved his hands down from her back to the dip of her waist, then down farther to the flare of her hips. She fit perfectly against him. He had no doubt he'd fit perfectly inside her, as well.

The sound of her sniffle broke him out of his very dangerous fantasies about them together.

He pulled back to a safer distance and studied her glassy eyes and adorably pink nose. "Don't worry. Between you, me and Amanda, we'll figure something out so you'll be able to get work and stay in California."

"I know." She shook her head even as she agreed with him. That was Gabby—always a little bit contrary. She swiped at her eyes. "I just can't seem to stop."

"You're over-tired. It's been a long night." And that's why he dropped his hands from her tempting body.

She nodded. "I didn't really sleep last night. I'd been too nervous about the trip to Tijuana."

Perhaps she should have listened to her instincts and not gone. He kept that thought to himself and instead tipped his head.

"Let's get you to bed." He watched her eyes flare. Shit. He did not need her to be interested in that, because he was having enough trouble keeping his own libido in check. He added quickly, "To sleep."

"Okay." This bold woman with an insecure side shifted her glance to and away from him, then back again. "Will you stay with me? To sleep. I'm afraid I won't be able to sleep with everything going on."

"Yeah. Sure." It was going to be torture, being in the same room with her for the rest of the night given the thoughts running through his head.

But he'd feel safer with her near him. There was still the unresolved matter of the drug cartel coming after their stash and possibly after her.

Looping an arm around her shoulder, he led her to the bedroom where they would just sleep, and nothing else.

That was definitely for the best.

Sex came with too many complications as it was. Sex with Gabby came with more than usual.

She was his sister's best friend. And he'd accepted now she wasn't going anywhere. She'd always be in his sister's life and by extension in his.

The aftermath of a one-night stand with her would make their inevitable reunion at the next gathering more than awkward.

So instead of taking off her clothes, Zach reached into the dresser and pulled out a shirt for her to put on. He thrust the extra-large US NAVY T-shirt toward her. "You can sleep in that if you want."

She stared at it for a second before she reached out and took it with a mumbled thanks. It seemed the poor tired thing was having trouble with even the most basic things.

"I'm gonna go brush my teeth. I'll leave a clean towel and a spare toothbrush in the bathroom for you."

"Thank you." Her eyes were glassy again, like she was going to cry over a toothbrush.

Yup, she was definitely over-tired. And thank God he'd gotten control of himself and hadn't kissed her.

"I'll be back in a few minutes." He backed out of the room and closed the door behind him before he decided to comfort her in so many inappropriate ways.

By the time he got back, she was sound asleep on top of the covers, the T-shirt reaching to her knees, which were tucked up as she curled into the fetal position.

Luckily his new decorating scheme was ripe with throw blankets. They might look nice draped all over the living room but until now he was wondering when the hell he'd ever use them.

He grabbed one and flipped it into the air, spreading it out and letting it settle over the bed and Gabby. He stripped quick and pulled on a pair of cotton drawstring shorts and crept under the throw next to her on the bed.

Definitely not how he'd pictured this night going, but as she sighed adorably in her sleep next to him he repeated his assertion, it could have been so much worse.

CHAPTER EIGHTEEN

Gabby opened her eyes and went stiff—but not as stiff as what she felt pressed against her.

Holy moly, she was in Zach's bed. And Zach's . . . *you know what* was jamming her in the back.

She reviewed the events of last night and tried to fill in the blanks. She remembered him handing her a US Navy T-shirt. The same kind of T-shirt he'd been wearing all those years ago when she'd first spied him walking into her dorm building before she'd even known who he was.

The same kind of shirt she'd dreamed of—literally—since then. And now she was wearing it.

But enough of that. Back to last night and how she ended up in Zach's bed with him—OMG—spooning her.

Last night she'd stripped out of her own clothes, which she'd been in for more than eighteen hours during her Tijuana fiasco, and pulled his T-shirt over her head.

She recalled noticing it smelled like her favorite Yankee Candle Company scent *Clean Cotton*.

They were one of the few splurges she allowed herself. Those candles weren't cheap and she rationed the number of hours she'd let herself burn one each night before bed. But she might have to stock up on more because she had a feeling she'd want to be reminded of this moment often.

She'd lain down on top of his bed, waiting for him to be done in the bathroom and that was the last thing she remembered.

Apparently she'd fallen asleep and he'd crawled into bed with her.

Definitely a dream come true. He'd even covered her with one of the throws she'd bought for the living room. The decorator inside her swelled with pride that he was using it.

But more than pride, was amazement. He could have slept in the other room, there was a bed in there, but he'd said he wouldn't leave her alone and he'd kept his promise.

Although the spooning was a bonus, and a very nice surprise.

A low groan from behind her had her holding her breath and trying not to move.

"Good morning." Zach's voice was gruff.

"Good morning. How did you—" She rolled over and came face to face with Zach and had trouble finishing her thought given the closeness. She swallowed hard. "How did you know I was awake?"

"Your breathing changed. Your movements were different." He lifted one shoulder. "I just felt it."

"Oh." What else could she say to that? She'd have to remember SEALs had super good senses.

Good thing he couldn't read minds too . . . she hoped.

She searched for a change of subject and spotted the lamp on the bedside table. She remembered the conversation from last night. "Nice lampshade."

The corner of his lips quirked up in a crooked smile. "Thanks."

Damn, he looked good in the morning. Which raised the question of how she looked.

She had a feeling it wasn't good. Since she'd fallen asleep with yesterday's make-up on, she probably had raccoon eyes from her mascara.

And God she hoped she didn't have morning breath to the tenth power since she'd never gotten to brush her teeth last night.

Scratch the dream come true part, because in her dreams of her and Zach she'd had fresh breath. And she'd looked breathtaking—at least that's what she'd imagined him saying to her.

"Coffee?" he asked, bringing her back to reality.

"Yes, please." And while they were back in reality, there were a few loose ends from last night she'd forgotten about.

Drug runners. The car she'd purposely left in Coronado for them to rob. The tile she hoped made it to the shop with the couple of SEALs who'd swooped in to the rescue.

Zach untangled himself from the throw and sat up. Sitting on the edge of the bed, he glanced back and frowned. "What's wrong?"

"How do you know something's wrong?"

He laughed. "You don't exactly have a poker face. I can see something is going on in that brain of yours. Something's bothering you. What is it?"

"I was just wondering about my car. And the drugs . . . And the tile."

"I'll check my cell. If there are no messages, I can make a few calls. Good?" he asked, his amusement at her random list of concerns evident.

"Perfect. Thank you."

"You're very welcome." He walked to the dresser and grabbed another T-shirt out of the drawer, pulling it over his head and hiding one of her favorite parts of him—those abs.

Then again, after this morning, she'd been up close and personal with another part of him that had felt pretty damn nice too. Of course, *that* part had faded the moment he woke up and his conscious self realized it was only her he was in bed with.

She sighed as he left the room. She heard the bathroom door close and waited for her turn. It opened again a couple of minutes later and she swung her legs out of bed.

It had been too long since she'd used a bathroom so she didn't take the time to change. She padded barefoot across the hall and took care of necessary business, before she allowed herself to look in the mirror.

It wasn't horrifying, but it wasn't great either. As he'd promised, Zach had left her a toothbrush and a towel. She brushed her teeth and scrubbed her face and did the best she could finger combing her hair.

Clean faced was the best she could do since her purse was somewhere out in the living room. And there was only lip gloss in there anyway. No makeup. She hadn't been planning a sleepover with a hot guy when she'd left Amanda's house yesterday morning.

Oh well. Zach was going to have to put up with her just the way she was. Not that he cared what she looked like anyway.

That was obvious since they'd been in bed together and he hadn't even made a move. Morning wood didn't count.

Resigned to the fact he wasn't attracted to her, she was about to go back into the bedroom and get dressed when the tantalizing aroma of fresh brewed coffee drifted to where she stood in the hall.

That temptation was accompanied with the sound of Zach speaking to somebody on the phone piqued her curiosity. She bypassed the bedroom door and headed for the kitchen.

Zach stood in the kitchen with the cell phone in one hand and the coffee pot in the other.

When he saw her he froze mid-pour. His gaze dropped down her body, from the T-shirt he'd loaned her, to her bare legs that the shirt didn't quite cover.

"Yeah, okay." He broke his gaze away from her to answer whoever was on the phone. "Understood. Thank you."

He lowered the cell and laid it on the counter.

"Coffee's ready," he said as he kept his gaze on her face this time.

"Great. Thanks." She grabbed her own phone out of the charging station and hit the button to wake it up as she moved toward the kitchen.

The screen filled with notifications—missed calls, texts and voicemails—all from Amanda.

Gabby drew in a breath and let it out in a sigh. "Your sister is blowing up my phone. Do we have any updates?"

His eyes were on the T-shirt again when she set her cell on the counter and glanced up at him.

He slid a coffee mug toward her. "Uh, yeah. Actually I do. First, there was a text from Hawk. Your tile is safe and sound inside the shop. He even sent a picture as proof."

She picked up the mug and smiled. "Hawk is a smart man. Please thank him for me."

"Will do. Next, though Silas was not happy with us for not following orders, he told me our friends from across the border did come and retrieve their boxes."

She swallowed a mouthful of coffee as her eyes widened. "Did they arrest them?"

Zach pressed his lips together. "He wouldn't say much but he said not to worry. They are on the case. My guess is they want bigger fish than a couple of low level couriers sent to grab the boxes, so they're probably tracking the delivery to the distributor. Oh, and he said your car is still at Compass's place and unharmed."

She shook her head in amazement. "Wow. It all worked out."

"Amazingly, it did." He cocked a brow. "But that doesn't mean you should plan on getting more of your decorating supplies from Mexico."

"Oh, don't worry. I'm done with that." Her gaze dropped to the steaming brew in her mug. "My business here is probably done too so . . ."

She shrugged and let the sentence trail off.

When she glanced up, Zach's gaze was on her face. She saw genuine concern etched in his features.

"You really think so?" he asked.

"Yeah. It's time to face reality and do the adult thing."

"I'm sorry."

She believed him. "I know. So am I."

"So what are you going to do?" he asked.

"Move back to Hawaii. My parents have a

beautiful house with plenty of space for me. It shouldn't make me feel so bad."

"But it does," he said.

"Yeah. It does."

"If there's anything I can do to help . . ."

Since he'd offered, she said, "Any chance I can keep this shirt? You know, as a memento of our night in Tijuana."

He laughed. "Yeah, sure."

"Thanks." God, she was going to miss her life in California. And Amanda. And Zach.

Didn't it figure? After over a decade of him hating her, when they finally reached a truce and he seemed to actually like her, she'd have to leave.

"Jesus, girl. You're breaking my heart looking so sad," he said, still watching her.

"I'm fine." She blinked back the mist in her eyes. Why did he have to be so sweet now?

He moved around the island and pulled her into his arms, surprising her.

It was a perfectly chaste hug. One between friends, which is what they seemed to have become, against all odds.

But then something changed. When she looked up at him, their faces were close. Oh so close.

It might have been him, or it might have been her, or maybe both of them at the same time, but that distance closed and his lips touched hers. So soft. So brief.

He pulled back just a fraction, watching her face. The unspoken question in his gaze asked did she want this?

Hell yeah, she wanted it.

Reaching up, she smashed her mouth against his.

CHAPTER NINETEEN

It was only about eight hours ago that he'd sworn this was a bad idea. That he should not kiss Gabrielle Lee. That his being with his sister's best friend made things too complicated.

What a difference a day made because he was sure kissing the fuck out of her now. It might be his worst decision ever, but he wasn't done with her yet. He was going in for more.

Angling his head, he thrust his tongue between her lips and dove into the hot wet heat of her mouth. She tasted of coffee and toothpaste.

At least her mouth did.

His mind went to bad places and he imagined tasting the rest of her. Running his tongue over her nipples before diving in between her legs.

A groan escaped him as his cock made its wishes known by stretching the too thin cotton of his shorts.

He hauled her tighter against him with one palm flattened at the small of her back. She pressed close, causing sweet agony as she trapped his erection between them.

Winding her massive length of hair around his

other hand, he tugged her head back so he could possess her mouth more fully. All while knowing kissing her wasn't going to be enough.

This had been a long time coming. He knew that.

It was just the first time he'd let himself admit it.

Was it eleven years ago he'd been at that frat party? Back when she'd been too young and too drunk, he'd managed to keep his hands off her and his thoughts about her in those short shorts mostly clean.

Eight or so years ago at his parents' pool, his body had gotten away from him, but he'd dealt with things on his own and put her out of his mind—mostly.

Until now.

Now she wasn't a kid anymore. They were both consenting adults.

He'd spent so many years trying to avoid her. Now he couldn't get close enough. The clothing between them, what little of it there was, seemed like too much.

She was still in his T-shirt and *fuck* did it look good on her. The easy access it afforded proved too tempting, so he didn't resist. He slid his hand down and then back up beneath the fabric.

Underwear covered her beneath the shirt. That was easily remedied. He slid his hand around to her stomach, then slipped a finger down beneath the elastic waistband.

He kissed her harder as his breath came faster.

Her skin was smooth and warm—and getting warmer the lower he went. When he slipped his finger between her folds, she felt downright hot.

She gasped at his touch. The sound was nearly his undoing.

When she moved her feet farther apart, it was all the invitation he needed. He hoisted her up with two hands on her waist and set her on the counter, narrowly missing their coffee mugs.

She pushed the breakables away then focused heavily-lidded eyes on his.

Those eyes widened as he bent low while pushing the shirt up to her waist. She fisted the fabric in one hand to hold it out of the way as she watched him.

With one hand braced on the countertop, she lifted up when he struggled to tug her underwear down her hips.

Then it was smooth sailing. He dropped her underwear to the floor and pushed her bare thighs wide.

Yup. Long time coming.

He'd imagined doing this when he'd been trying to fall asleep next to her last night.

And if he were honest with himself, he'd have to admit he'd pictured this years ago while jerking off in the bathroom during the pool party.

Dipping his head low, he held her wide with his thumbs and plunged his tongue between them.

She cried out at first contact, which only encouraged him to work harder.

He wanted to hear her come.

More than that, he wanted to hear her cry out his name. To know, to remember forever, that it was him who made her come so hard she couldn't control herself.

And where was all this coming from? This possessiveness. This need to claim her. Mark her. Sear memories of them into her mind so she'd be ruined for all other men even if there could soon be an ocean between them.

He had to be feeling like this because she said she was thinking of leaving.

Irony was a bitch.

When she was around all the time, all he wanted was for her to go away.

Now, she hadn't even left yet and he was already anticipating the enormous suck of being thousands of miles from her.

He attacked his mission with renewed vigor until she started to shake.

He'd make her come, then make her his. At least his for the day. He hoped she had no other plans today because he might not be satisfied with one time.

It might take until lunch to satisfy this craving—possibly through dinner.

Gabby gasped. He felt as she crested, peaking loud and hard as she thrust against his mouth.

After feeling that, his sole goal was to get inside her.

The counter was definitely too high for fucking. The sofa was an option but the bed was preferable by far. Nice and big with plenty of room to get creative.

"Bedroom?" he asked, incapable of more than the single word.

"Good idea," she whispered.

He liked Gabby when she was soft spoken and agreeable. But then again, he was starting to not mind when she was rambling.

Somehow she had gone from annoying to amusing the more he got to know her.

And Christ, she was too frigging tempting to resist for a second longer.

Zach hoisted her off the counter. She wrapped her

arms and legs around him and he carried her the short distance to the bedroom.

He tumbled her onto the bed, and had to resist the temptation to crawl on top of her. There was the matter of protection he had to deal with first.

Luckily he'd stocked up on all the necessities after getting back—milk, eggs, condoms.

Maybe this happening between them wasn't such a surprise after all. Given he'd prepared for it when he'd been at the store, could he subconsciously have been anticipating this happening between them from the moment he found her in his shower?

He certainly hadn't known she'd be so tempting in his T-shirt—or that she'd have opportunity to be wearing it at all—but the tension between them had been there all along.

Possibly since that first night of the frat party.

Resigned this had for sure been a long time coming and pocketing any residual guilt he still felt for wanting his little sister's best friend so badly, he pulled open the drawer and reached inside for the brand new box of condoms.

"You're using the table I got you." She smiled.

If that he was using her table was what she was most happy about right now, he'd better up his sexual game.

He intended to make her forget all about the table, and all the other stuff in here she'd fished out of the trash and put in his bedroom.

This woman . . . He shook his head at how she could drive him mad, and then the time for thinking was done.

"Yeah, I'm using it," he said as he dropped his drawers.

That did it. Her focus went immediately to the cock bobbing between them as he sheathed himself.

As he moved toward the bed, she raised her gaze from his dick to his eyes.

He saw her kaleidoscope of emotions as her face cycled through a full repertoire of expressions. Trepidation, disbelief . . . desire.

He was feeling a few of those same things himself. Maybe they weren't so different.

As he crawled onto the mattress she moved over to make space for him. He didn't want space. He wanted her.

With both hands, he spread her legs and moved between them, and then he took her. He plunged inside Gabby like he'd been made to fit inside this woman.

His spine bowed as he thrust deep. The arms he'd braced on either side of her shook with the sensation of being squeezed inside her tight wet heat and he bit out a curse filled with amazement.

The feel of her hands clutching at his ass and urging him to move brought him out of his own head. He opened the eyes he hadn't realized he'd slammed shut and glanced down at Gabby.

Lips parted, breath shallow, she was breathtaking as her gaze met his and he couldn't resist leaning low and taking her lips.

He made love to her mouth as he set a slow steady rhythm with his hips. The cadence sped and soon turned frantic, through no fault of his own.

As Gabby lifted her hips and started to cry out Zach couldn't maintain any semblance of control.

His new goal was to drive her over the edge into a body rocking orgasm while he was inside her.

When it started to happen, he thought he'd lose his mind.

Her body locked down around his, squeezing him.

He held on as long as he could, which wasn't long. The pleasure ran down his spine and right through his balls as he exploded inside her.

The pulses of his climax matched hers as she wrung him dry, body and soul.

He collapsed over her, panting and calculating how soon they could do it again as, semi-hard, he twitched inside her with aftershocks. He pressed closer against her and she drew in a sharp breath, letting it out on a sigh.

That did it. He was growing, nearly hard again, like he was a teenager. He pulled out, snapped off the used condom and tore into a new one, thinking he probably should have gotten the economy-sized box rather than the small one.

He rolled it on and plunged back inside as Gabby, looking boneless beneath him, pressed her head back against the pillow.

She opened her eyes and the pools of chocolate brown captured him—until he surged inside again and those eyes squeezed shut.

Pulling out, he watched and waited, and she didn't disappoint him. She opened those eyes again and caught his gaze.

A tip of his hips forward as his hands held her off the bed and he hit the spot he sought. Her eyes rolled back. He tried the move again, pulling out, catching her gaze, then plunging back inside to hit her G-spot.

As he'd hoped, her eyes rolled back again and he let out a laugh of pure glee.

Sex was always satisfying. After all, coming was

coming. But sex with Gabby was—fun. There was no other way to put it, and he liked it.

"I'm not sure I like you laughing at me during this." Her eyes were open now, and narrowed as she glared at him while he smiled.

"I can't help it. Every time I bump right there." He nudged the spot in question to demonstrate. "Your eyes roll back in your head. Just like that." He grinned wider.

"Oh, yeah?" She slid her hands across the globes of his ass and yanked his hips forward, pulling him deeper inside her. "Later, I'm going to make your eyes roll back in your head and laugh at you."

If she wanted to punish him, promising to torture him sexually wasn't the way to do it.

"If that is a threat, it's not working because that sounds pretty damn good to me." He started to imagine all the many ways she could torture him and his balls began to tingle.

No more games. No more laughing. He couldn't resist the urge to pump into her until he drove himself to a second climax.

This time when he collapsed, he wasn't sure he could get up. He had patrolled sixty-miles in mountainous enemy territory in full kit and not felt as drained as he did now. Certainly not this satisfied.

A nice nap with Gabby's breasts as his pillow while her heartbeat lulled him to sleep might be in order.

And then her stomach growled.

A smile twitched on his lips. "Hungry?"

"Yes. Sorry."

"Don't apologize." Rest time was over.

He needed to feed his woman—so he could work

up her appetite again later.

Zach pushed off the mattress. "Want to stay here and I'll grab us something quick?"

"Sure." She was pink-cheeked and adorable in his bed and he didn't want to leave. But he was hungry too.

One thing he was sure of was it was going to be a quick meal, because he wasn't going to spend his morning in the kitchen while Gabby was in his bed.

Two minutes later, he came back with bowls of cereal and a couple of spoons.

He paused next to the bed where she lay making his shirt look good. "There's not much in the house. I didn't stock up on a lot food because I wasn't planning on hanging around here."

"Why not?" she asked. "It's not a bad place to hang out."

"I was afraid I'd be bored." He raised his gaze to hers. "Then you showed up."

She lifted her brows. "Is that a compliment? I can't tell."

"It's a fact. Now sit up and eat before your flakes get soggy."

"Yes, sir." After a comically messy salute, she did as told, hoisting herself up against the pillows and folding her legs in front of her.

"Don't call me sir. I'm enlisted, not an officer." He thrust one bowl at her, then set his down on the table so he could get situated himself.

"And I have no idea what the difference is so . . ." She lifted a shoulder and slurped milk and flakes off her spoon.

Grabbing his own bowl, he laughed. "At least I know you're not a frog hog . . ." At her blank expression he added, "That's a woman who actively tries to sleep with Navy SEALs."

"I don't know about that. I might be one. You had me at your US NAVY T-shirt."

"The one you're wearing?" he asked.

If as a recruit years ago he'd known giving a girl a NAVY T-shirt was the sure way to get her into bed, he probably would have blown his whole month's pay at the base exchange buying them by the case.

"No." She shook her head. "The shirt you were wearing when you came to visit Amanda our freshman year. Remember?" she asked.

He let out a laugh. "Yeah, I remember." He'd never forget.

He'd stayed to chaperone that damn frat party to protect his sister from her wild roommate. But looking back, he had to wonder who was leading who when it came to the college party life—Amanda or Gabby.

Knowing Gabby better now, and having known his rebellious-minded sister Amanda's whole life, Zach had a feeling he'd misinterpreted that whole situation.

They sat on the bed, legs folded beneath them, knees touching between them as they both slurped milk and flakes off soup spoons. Her face scrubbed clean of makeup. Her hair loose and messy from sleep—and sex. His T-shirt swallowing her curves. She was nothing like he'd imagined she would be.

He liked Gabby and he wasn't quite sure what to do with that feeling.

His opinion of her might have changed, but their situation hadn't. Amanda was still her friend and his sister.

Just doing what they'd already done would make things awkward going forward.

And if they tried to take this to the next level and failed, it would put Amanda in the middle between them. In the impossible position of having to take sides and choose either her best friend or her brother.

Next level. What the hell was he thinking?

His leave would end and he'd go back to being one hundred percent focused on the team. And she'd already mentioned moving back to Hawaii.

There might be a tomorrow for the two of them— and another night or even a few together—but after next week there was no time left for them. No next month. No next level.

Maybe that was a good thing. Right now, he couldn't decide.

Either way, the situation was what it was and he didn't have the power to change any of it.

CHAPTER TWENTY

"I know you two talk about everything but please, for both of our sakes, not a word to Amanda about what happened between you and me." There was pleading in Zach's tone.

"I won't tell. I promise."

He cocked up one brow, looking skeptical as they walked from his truck in the driveway toward Amanda's door.

They'd been summoned there this morning because Amanda demanded an explanation of everything that had happened last night in detail and in person.

Luckily she wasn't an early riser so her texts to both Zach and Gabby's phones, followed by a call when they didn't reply right away, had come after their insane sex.

Insanely good. Insanely unexpected.

She might have dreamed about Zach like that for years but to have it really happen—she was still pinching herself to make sure she wasn't dreaming.

Maybe she had died at the hands of the drug lords last night and this was her life now in heaven.

Not so bad if that was the deal. Sex like she'd had this morning with Zach for all of eternity? She could live with that—so to speak.

But no, this was no dream or heaven, because Zach was scowling at her.

She shot him a glare. "I'm not going to tell her."

He still didn't look happy.

Fine. That made two of them. She was a little pissy herself because he wouldn't let her get her car back from that SEAL's garage. He said the drug dealers could have messed with it. Put a tracker on it to come and get her later to tie up loose ends. Or put explosives in it to blow her up when she opened the door or started the ignition.

It was ridiculous.

She watched a lot of TV and she'd seen all those plotlines, but that kind of stuff didn't happen to her.

Then again, she'd never imagined drugs being planted in her tile boxes either so maybe she wasn't the best judge of what was or was not normal anymore.

She wasn't allowed near the car until his SEAL buddy got the government dude to check it out—at least that's what she'd taken away from his explanation to her. He'd spewed out all these names and she couldn't keep track of who was who.

It didn't matter anyway. Unless she stole his truck or ordered a ride to Coronado she was at his mercy, riding shotgun in his pick-up. And if she asked Amanda for a ride, he'd really lose his mind at her defying his orders and putting his sister in jeopardy—

real or imagined.

Nope. She'd finally gotten on Zach's good side and she intended to stay there.

The orgasms were too good to risk losing.

They'd reached the door Amanda would be flinging open any second and he was still looking unhappy.

Gabby stopped and planted one hand on her hip. "Zachary Browne, stop frowning at me or Amanda is going to know for sure something is wrong. Then it will be your fault, not mine."

His lips twitched with a controlled smile.

"What?" she demanded.

"First, Amanda will think it's perfectly normal if I'm frowning at you. And second, you're cute when you're mad and stomp your foot like a little kid."

"I did not stomp—" Her denial was interrupted by the jiggle of the door lock just before Amanda tugged it open and glared at both of them. "Oh, my God. About time you got here. I've been dying. Come inside."

Zach shot Gabby one more warning look. She rolled her eyes and followed Amanda inside.

"I have a fresh pot of coffee on and cinnamon rolls just out of the oven."

"At least there's food," Zach grumbled before he moved past Amanda and headed for the cabinet where the mugs were.

Amanda always did like to cater an event— whether that be a party or a retelling of their night in Tijuana.

While Zach was busy at the coffeemaker, Amanda pulled Gabby into a hug. "I was so worried."

Gabby let out a short laugh. "So was I . . . for

awhile." Until Zach showed up.

She pulled out of the embrace and glanced at Zach. Her savior. She forced her focus back to Amanda and saw her friend's eyes narrow.

Amanda glanced from Gabby to Zach and back again before her eyes shot wide. "Oh my God. You two did it."

"What?" Gabby drew back, shocked.

Her gaze shot to Zach as he turned from the counter, coffee pot in one hand. He glared back at her.

Gabby held up her hands, palms forward. "I didn't tell her. I swear."

"Oh my God, it's true. You did do it," Amanda squealed.

Apparently all Gabby's denial had done was add fuel to the fire of Amanda's suspicions.

Lips pressed tight, Zach set down the coffee pot and pointed to his sister. "One more word and I walk out of here right now and don't come back."

"My lips are sealed." Amanda ran her fingers across her mouth like she was zipping her lips shut.

Gabby watched with amazement.

Interesting tactic he'd chosen. Not a denial, just a threat. And it worked—for now.

Amanda had already broken out into a smile as she kept looking between the two of them but at least there was no commentary—it must be killing Amanda to not say anything.

Gabby had a feeling she'd be getting an earful later though, as soon as Zach was out of earshot.

Stone-faced, Zach delivered Gabby a cup of coffee, fixed just the way she liked it. Amanda reacted with two raised brows and her mouth pressed tight as if she were physically trying to hold in the words.

He spun to his sister with that pointer finger out again. "Not. One. Word."

Her eyes went wide with feigned innocence. "What? I didn't say a thing."

"Yeah, whatever." Zach grumbled as he made his way back to get his own mug. He stayed there on the other side of the kitchen and waited, silent, spreading his glare between them.

Gabby assumed that was her cue to start the retelling. She might not be all that great at keeping her mouth shut but she was exceptionally good at talking.

That Zach was seemingly embracing that fact seemed like a good sign and a huge step forward.

Now if she could only remember what she was and was not allowed to tell Amanda about last night. Crap.

CHAPTER TWENTY-ONE

After a week of lying next to Gabby all night every night, he was used to her habits.

Zach knew to hang on tight to his half of the covers or she'd steal them all.

He knew she'd curl up on her side in a little ball when she was really tired, but by the middle of the night she'd be sprawled spread eagle across three quarters of the bed. He knew every once in a while she'd make the most adorable little snore that would sometimes wake her.

And he knew that anytime he reached for her she snuggled against him and didn't mind at all if the reason he'd tugged her closer was because he couldn't wait until morning to have her.

He was exhausted from his time off.

His leave was supposed to be for him to get rest and relaxation, possibly on a sandy beach or a secluded hunting cabin. Or for wild times of drinking or gambling, perhaps in Vegas. And—after being celibate for way too long thanks to his deployment—this leave was for him to catch up on sex. Lots of sex.

One out of three wasn't bad.

But now, as the glow of sunrise crept through the blinds, he needed to get up. He had no intention of having his sister bust into Gabby's room and find him there naked.

In hindsight, he should have sucked it up, stopped drinking after dinner last night and driven the two of them back to his house.

It would have been worth it. When they had privacy Gabby could be quite . . . *vocal* in bed.

Last night she'd done her best to be quiet. And he had the teeth marks on his chest where she'd bitten him in an attempt to stay silent when she came.

At the memory, he absently rubbed at the spot.

His lips quirked with a smile. Okay, maybe he hadn't hated that part. Not at all.

He padded barefoot around the room, finding his pants and shirt in the near darkness to not wake Gabby. He hated he had to get dressed in last night's clothes just so he could go to his sister's kitchen to get coffee.

Was this the male version of the walk of shame? He'd no doubt get shit about it from his sister.

He knew he was in trouble when he quietly opened the bedroom door and got the first whiff of the aroma of fresh coffee brewing drifting down the hallway.

Bracing himself for whatever Amanda had to throw at him, he eased the bedroom door closed and made his way to the kitchen.

"Good morning." Her expression said so much more than her words.

So glad he could amuse her. "Morning." Eyes down he walked around the kitchen island and said,

"Coffee ready?"

"Just about." She drew in a breath and he knew he was in trouble. "So you go from not wanting me to know about you two at all, to staying overnight here?"

"I drank too much last night to drive home. It was safer to stay here."

She tipped her head. "Yes, it was. And it wasn't like you were fooling anyone anyway. She's slept at your house every night since Tijuana."

Zach didn't need that reminder at all. His ill-advised one-night stand had gone on for over a week now.

It shouldn't have happened the first time. It really shouldn't have been repeated. Over and over and over again.

He blamed it on his denying himself for so long. He had a lot of missed sex to make up for. That was his theory and he was sticking to it, in spite of the nagging voice in the back of his mind calling him a liar.

Zach lifted one shoulder, not willing to get into the specifics of his sex life or his feelings about Gabby with his sister at all, never mind pre-coffee.

It was bad enough they'd had to do it under her roof last night.

That concept was disturbing in and of itself. But obviously not disturbing enough to make him not want to have sex with Gabby.

"So, you two are pretty serious, I guess," Amanda continued.

"No." The denial came out with more force than he'd intended.

She blew out a loud breath. "How can you say that?"

"Easy. My leave is up tomorrow. And once I'm back on duty, you know what it's like. I'm away all the time, sometimes on short notice, sometimes for long stretches."

"Gabby knows that. We've been friends for as long as you've been a SEAL."

He certainly didn't need that reminder either.

Gabby and Amanda's close, long-standing friendship was one of the things that sat dead center in his consciousness, nagging him during every waking moment.

He needed a nice dangerous mission to get his head back on straight. Having free time obviously wasn't working for him.

Tired of waiting for the full pot of coffee to finish brewing, he grabbed the carafe and splashed coffee into one of the mugs on the counter, before shoving it back under the dripping brown liquid.

He shot a glance at his sister as he reached for the cream. "Knowing what being with a team guy is like and living it are two different things. It's best if we keep this casual."

"Casual." She let out a snort. "Does she know this plan? Have you discussed it with her?"

"Well, not in so many words . . ." Talking in general wasn't high on his list of favorite activities.

Talking about feelings and shit was even lower.

Amanda's brow shot high. She had the most judgmental frigging eyebrows he'd ever encountered.

Well, maybe not. He remembered his mother shooting him a similar look when she'd caught him sneaking in at dawn when he was sixteen.

Must be hereditary on the female side of the family.

"I'll handle it. Okay?" He raised the mug to his lips, hoping this was the end of the conversation.

"No, it's not okay. Because when you leave and are having a high old time running the O-Course on Coronado or whatever it is you guys do all day, I'll be here alone with Gabby trying to heal her broken heart because you dumped her."

He couldn't help but smile at the ridiculousness of it all. *Broken heart.* After a little over a week of sex?

His sister had been watching too many chick flicks. He should probably tell his brother-in-law to round up and burn all those romance novels he saw laying around the house too.

"You saying I'm a heartbreaker, sis?" he joked to avoid this conversation. She was being too serious and ruining his morning.

Amanda wasn't laughing. "Gabby isn't the kind to sleep around. She's had a handful of serious relationships and I know for a fact her *number* as you guys like to call it, is a tenth of what yours is."

"What do you know about my number?" He had to step to the side so Amanda could wipe up the dripped coffee on the counter.

She sent him a glare and tossed the sponge into the sink. "I know things."

The frightening part was, he believed her. He wouldn't put it past Amanda to have a network of spies and know about every woman he'd ever been with.

"Jesus," he blew out the curse. This woman scared him sometimes.

"Look, all I'm saying is don't hurt her. She's been in love with you for years. She deserves better than that."

Love. The word echoed through his brain.

He frowned at his sister. "Love is a bit of a stretch, don't you think?"

Yes, Gabby had looked at him with her doe eyes over the years, but that was a schoolgirl crush at best. They were adults now. Capable of fulfilling each other's physical needs with no strings attached.

Amanda screwed up her mouth and shot him a sideways glare. "You are so clueless, I swear."

"Good morning." The sound of Gabby's voice brought his head around.

He couldn't help but smile at how she could look so cute and sexy swimming in the loose navy blue cotton.

She'd taken to wearing his T-shirt to sleep every night. He, of course, loved the easy access it provided to her body.

Best thing he'd ever done was give that shirt to her.

"Good morning," he said and turned to reach for the carafe to pour her a cup of coffee.

"Good morning," Amanda said. Something in her tone had Zach turning to glance at her as she continued, "So, what big plans do you have for Zach's last day of leave before he goes back on duty tomorrow?"

"Tomorrow?"

His gaze shot to Gabby's face. She was visibly taken aback.

"Didn't you know?" Amanda asked Gabby, before she turned to look at him, brows raised and full of accusation.

Dammit.

Zach focused on Gabby. "I told you. Remember

that first day you were at my house. I told you I was on leave for two weeks and you'd better be done with my house by then."

"I don't remember." She shook her head, looking devastated and unsure. "But if today is your last day off, you probably have a ton of stuff you have to do on your own."

"I don't really," he said, his chest tightening as her eyes got glassy. "We can hang out today."

"Actually, I have work to do on the shop. She's got a soft opening next week and I haven't finished all the staging yet."

There was no excitement in her voice, the way there usually was when she talked about work. And this was the first time she'd said no to their spending time together.

Shit. Amanda could be right.

He didn't know what the fuck to do with that knowledge or with the sudden tightness in his chest.

But he knew one thing. He wasn't going to let her keep looking at him like that with hurt in her eyes.

He took a step forward and pulled her toward him, ignoring Amanda's presence. That she didn't come willingly right into his embrace, like she usually did, was harder to ignore.

"If you have stuff to do for the shop, then I'll come with you."

She shook her head, feeling stiff beneath his hands. "You don't have to—"

"I want to," he cut her off.

She hesitated, then finally raised her eyes to meet his gaze. "Okay."

Satisfied, he nodded. Today was taken care of. He'd worry about tomorrow, tomorrow.

Jasper walked out of the bedroom, freshly showered and dressed for work.

"Good morning, everyone." His gaze moved over the solemn group assembled in the kitchen as he headed toward the coffeemaker. Oblivious to the mood hanging over the room, he asked, "So what're everyone's plans on this fine day?"

Zach let out a sniff. Maybe Amanda was right about that too—men were clueless. Himself included.

CHAPTER TWENTY-TWO

Gabby stared at her phone, willing it to ring, or chime, or something. Anything. It hadn't done any of the above all day. In fact, she'd gotten no texts or calls since she'd left Zach's house last night.

Bastard.

"Talk." Amanda demanded. "What's wrong."

"Nope." Gabby shook her head.

"Why not?"

"Because I don't want to bad-mouth your brother to you."

Amanda waved away that concern. "Oh, please. I of all people know him well enough to know he deserves whatever you want to say about him, so spill."

Gabby made the split second decision to share. Amanda was her best friend as much as Zach's sister. And she needed her friend right now.

"So last night we spent, uh, time together." She cringed at having to allude to sex with Zach to Amanda but it was an important part of the story. "And then right after he says he has to be on base early the next morning."

He hadn't actually said *get the hell out of my bed*, but he might as well have. She'd gotten dressed, let him kiss her goodnight—but did not actively participate in the kiss—and then drove to Amanda's.

Last night she'd been torn between anger and tears. But after a full day of not even one text, she was just plain mad.

Amanda nodded. "He's an ass. No doubt about it. But in his defense I know he does leave for base insanely early. Like before dawn. He probably didn't want to wake you that early."

He'd woken her plenty early for sex all damn week. Gabby bit her tongue and kept that to herself.

"There's more to it than just that. He didn't even tell me his leave was over until you brought it up. Okay, maybe he did mention it like two weeks ago but you'd think it would have come up at least once over the week we spent sweaty in his bed. He could have, you know, maybe said, hey, thanks for the amazing sex and by the way my leave is over Monday."

"He's forgetful." Amanda cringed. "And a little less vivid visuals about my brother in bed, please."

Forgetful. Yup. He'd forgotten all about her already apparently.

Gabby continued, not inclined to worry too much about Amanda's sensitivities since she kept insisting on defending her brother's bad behavior. "You know why he didn't tell me, right? He didn't want to have *the talk*."

"What talk?"

"*The* talk. The, 'What is this? What are we?' talk. Where we decide if we're in a relationship or not.

Obviously, the answer is *not*."

Was he just going to ghost her? She might have been better off when he hated her. At least she knew what to expect from him then.

This—this on again, off again—was horrible.

"I'm not going to defend him, but I really do think he's just clueless when it comes to relationships, like most men. I think if you want your relationship defined, you have to define it. You need to tell him what you want to be to each other."

That sounded like the most frightening prospect Gabby had ever heard. "And what if he doesn't agree with what I want?"

Amanda shrugged. "Only one way to find out."

Easy for her to say. Gabby's heart began to pound just thinking about initiating this conversation with Zach.

She shook her head. "I don't know if I can do this."

"Gabby, you're a strong woman."

"No, I'm not." She shook her head.

Did her best friend not know her at all? She spent a dozen years with a crush on Zach and never once told him. That was not the actions of a strong woman.

"You survived your Tijuana adventure and got the job done. Beautifully, I might add."

She would agree, when it came to getting things done for work, she could kick some serious ass. But sadly, that wasn't enough.

Gabby let out a sigh. "It doesn't matter though. That job hasn't gotten me any new ones."

"It might once she opens the shop."

"I don't know about that. I've been posting the

whole thing on my blog and even doing some live stuff on IGTV on Instagram and nothing. Not one nibble. And the worst part is, even with driving to Mexico to get the tile cheaper, I still don't think I made any money on the shop."

Amanda frowned. "That can't be possible."

"I'm afraid it is. I bid real close to my margin so she'd be happy and recommend me to all her friends, and I didn't make hardly anything."

"Get me your receipts. I'm going to look at it for you."

Amanda, as a CPA, might be able to get a more detailed cost versus profit analysis than Gabby, but that wouldn't change the end result.

After all the unexpected expenses and the amount of time it had taken her, the profit she'd hoped would be enough to set her up in a nice apartment and keep her rolling along until new jobs came pouring in just wasn't there.

Especially since there were no new jobs pouring in. Not even a trickle.

Amanda stood and said, "Go get your paperwork. I'll get my laptop and go over your numbers . . . while you call Zach."

"What?" Gabby's eyes popped wide. "Nuh, uh."

"Do it." Amanda folded her arms.

Gabby had been up against that stubborn look before. There was no winning.

She let out a huff. "Fine."

Her only consolation was that Amanda wasn't in for an easy night either. She knew that as she hoisted her overstuffed tote bag off the floor with a grunt. It contained her entire business life, in no order whatsoever.

She plopped it on the table in front of Amanda with a thud.

"All my receipts are in there." Satisfied that would suitably punish her friend for the torture Amanda was inflicting by making her call Zach, Gabby reached for her cell.

She scrolled through the contacts in her list to find Zach's number. She couldn't go to recent calls or the text log because, surprise, surprise, he'd never texted or called her.

Zach really was a terrible communicator when she wasn't right there in the same room with him.

She hadn't realized that until now. Probably because they'd been together so much. Finishing his house. Running from drug lords. Having multiple orgasms.

God, she missed that. All of it. Even the bad stuff, because at least they'd been together for it.

She had it bad. And she was going to be a mess if this was over.

With a mixture of hope and dread, she called his number. It was past dinnertime. He must be done at the base by now, right?

Then again, what did she know? As he'd said, she was no frog log . . . or was it hog? Which was a very unflattering reference.

As her mind spun it was becoming obvious he wasn't going to answer. When his voicemail prompt came on—the computer generated one, not even his own voice—she hung up.

"No answer."

Amanda glanced up from the pile of papers on the table. "He's probably out running or something. Send a text instead and he'll get back to you when he can."

"Fine." Gabby opened a new text. "And what am I saying in this text?"

"That you'd like to talk."

"That should scare him away nicely." Gabby scowled, punching in the message.

"Oh ye of little faith."

Yup. That was her. Amanda had nailed her in one but she hit *send* on the text anyway and then walked to the counter.

If she was going to have to wait for Zach to get back to her, possibly forever, she might as well have a glass of wine while she did it.

"Want some wine?" she asked Amanda.

"No thanks."

"Really?" She frowned. That was odd.

"I'm working. Can't drink and calculate."

Gabby laughed. "I can't even calculate sober so I can respect that."

Glass in hand, Gabby settled in to wait it out. The wine could only help soften the blow of what she was sure would be bad news.

Gabby's glass was empty by the time Amanda made it through the pile of papers she'd dumped out of the bag and onto the table.

When everything was in neat little stacks, Amanda glanced up. From her expression alone, Gabby knew the news wasn't good.

"That bad?" she asked.

Amanda drew in a breath and let it out. "Well, you didn't lose money."

"That's good."

"But you didn't make a whole lot either." She turned the computer to face Gabby.

After a few seconds she found the bottom line of

the spreadsheet. The number for profit was far less than she'd hoped.

"For your first job, a thousand dollars isn't bad."

She sighed. It wasn't bad, but it wasn't enough.

"But I think I have some good news for you," Amanda continued.

"What's that?" Gabby asked, wondering if more wine would help or just depress her further. Drinking alone wasn't fun.

"I can give you another decorating job," Amanda said.

"No." Gabby shook her head. "I'm not letting you keep making up jobs for me."

"I'm not making it up. I really need you to decorate the spare room."

"For what?" she asked, not believing her friend.

"To be a nursery."

Gabby's gaze whipped to her friend. "You're pregnant?"

"Yup."

"Oh my God. That's so great." Tears in her eyes, she jumped up and ran around the table to hug Amanda. "But now I really can't stay here with you any longer."

"Don't be ridiculous. First of all, I have like eight more months before the baby comes. Second, you're going to be here anyway, decorating the nursery—"

"Which I'm not going to charge you for," Gabby interjected.

"We'll see about that," Amanda countered. "And third, I want you here. How great is it living together again, just like in college?"

It did sound great, but reverting back to the simpler times when she was carefree and eighteen wasn't going to solve her adult issues.

"Promise you'll stay," Amanda begged.

"I'll stay . . . for now." Defeated, it was easier to agree even if she did plan on leaving the minute the nursery was done.

She needed some privacy to search for flights without Amanda seeing. Gabby began gathering the piles, trying her best to keep the papers in the painstaking order Amanda had placed them in.

"But tonight, I'm beat. I know Jasper is working late, but would you mind if I go to sleep early?" she asked.

"Not at all. You go ahead. I want to finish my book anyway."

Gabby smiled. It might be a fictional heroine in a romance novel, but at least someone would be getting a happy ending tonight.

In her room, she changed for bed. She couldn't bring herself to put on Zach's T-shirt. The reminder of him hurt too much. So she pulled out her old flannel bottoms and a tank top and crawled into bed to check her cell.

No reply to her text. No surprise.

That was all the hints she needed from him. He'd ghosted her.

It was better this way. She knew what she had to do.

She'd finish Amanda's nursery this week and then head to Hawaii on the first flight she could get a reservation for that didn't cost an arm and a leg.

No jobs. No apartment. No boyfriend. Zach being out of her life would only make it easier to leave California.

There was nothing keeping her here, except for

her best friend. That part would be hard.

But Amanda would be busy with her new baby before she knew it. And maybe Gabby could save her money and use her frequent flier miles to come back and visit after the baby was born.

It would be fine.

With a sigh, she opened her computer and navigated to the travel booking site to start looking at options.

As the search results loaded she picked up the phone and scrolled through, hitting one contact.

She listened to the ringing as the dread built within her.

Finally, the ringing stopped, replaced by, "Aloha."

"Aloha, Mama." Gabby forced brightness into her voice as she said, "Guess what?"

CHAPTER TWENTY-THREE

"Training on the day we get back from leave. What the fuck? I swear they do this shit on purpose. The sadists." T-Bone tossed his bag onto the floor to unlock his cage.

Zach couldn't agree more. Coming back from two weeks off to an unannounced week long training in the Nevada dessert where cell signal was as elusive as hot running water had been an unwelcome surprise.

"Trial by fire. We needed to see how the new guys perform with the team before we go out on a real op," Justus pointed out.

"Better a fuck up here than in, say, Yemen," Nitro pointed out.

"True that. Wouldn't want anyone screwing up and getting shot in the ass or anything." Rocket's lips twitched with the joke.

Zach knew the reason they'd had the training. It didn't mean he liked it.

Though he could appreciate the slam against Dutch for getting shot in the ass last mission. Poor guy was never going to live that down.

But the training was done and he didn't have to be back on base for two whole days because, sadists or not, at least command had cut them a break now.

He was happy he could take a hot shower and get something to eat that didn't come in a bag. And, finally, he could take the time to sift through the multitude of texts and voicemails he'd gotten in his week off the grid.

His mom and dad had called and left a voicemail, of course. They called weekly to check in since they'd retired to Arizona.

There was a message from Hawk, plus a couple of funny gifs and memes Compass had texted to the team as a group.

He found only one text from Gabby, but enough from Amanda to make up for the shortage. He figured Gabby probably hadn't wanted to bother him so she had Amanda text him instead. He smiled at the thought.

She was so cute. He'd missed her during his week away.

Being in the desert had given him lots of time to think. Time away from her tempting body and adorable smile so he could evaluate things a little more clearly.

Maybe he was ready to get serious after all. To see where this thing with her might go.

His hesitation because she was Amanda's friend was a moot point now.

They'd spent too much time tangled up together to ignore it had happened so things were going to be awkward whether he dated her and they eventually broke up, or he'd never dated her at all.

And with his sister by her side for support, maybe

Gabby could handle the kind of life he lived as a SEAL.

There was a reason every man on the team was currently single, however, he also knew plenty of guys who had girlfriends, wives, kids—sometimes the relationship even survived.

This was definitely a conversation he needed to have with Gabby in person. And though he wasn't at all opposed to the idea of video chat sex with her while he was deployed, there was something else he'd like to do with her in person.

With that motivation, he showered and changed on base. Then grabbed his truck and headed for his sister's house.

It was just about dinnertime. Perfect. He'd get a meal out of the visit too.

Family. Good food. His woman. Everything he could want after a tough week of training. Yeah, he could get used to this.

Happy with his plan he headed directly to Amanda's rather than stopping by his empty house.

Sure, Gabby had made his house nice. Beautiful. Magazine-worthy actually. But people made a house a home. Not things.

The first thing he noticed when he pulled up to his sister's was that Gabby's car wasn't in the drive.

That had him cutting the engine and jumping from the truck to stride to the house.

The car, and Gabby, and now his sister and her husband, were all on the radar of some pretty nasty people and Zach didn't know Silas Branson enough to trust the DHS to keep everyone safe from blowback.

Sure, maybe she was working late at a design job.

But maybe she wasn't. He pounded on the door with his left hand while trying the knob with his right. It was locked.

He was about to reach for his cell phone. If no one answered the door or the phone, he wasn't above kicking the door in.

What most homeowners didn't realize was how shockingly easy it was to force your way through a locked door. The lock might be metal but the door holding it was nothing but wood. Usually pretty flimsy wood at that.

And why hadn't he thought of that before? He needed to beef up his sister's security. Even if everything turned out to be fine, he'd do it tomorrow.

He heard the jigging of the lock and Amanda telling him to wait a second.

She yanked open the door, frowning. "What's wrong? Why are you pounding like a maniac?"

"You tell me. Is everything okay?" he asked, glancing past her into the house, which was neat and clean as usual.

"Yes, why wouldn't it be?" she asked.

He had given her enough information about their Tijuana trip to make her cautious, but not enough to scare her.

She didn't realize his worst fear was that the drug ring would come after them all in retaliation for the DHS taking them down. *If* the DHS had done anything at all except trail them. Who knew? He'd been kept completely out of the loop. It was infuriating.

Fucking Branson.

"Where's Gabby's car?" he asked.

"For now, it's in my garage, behind my car."

"Why? What's wrong?" Was the drug cartel looking for her car and she had to hide it?

"Nothing's wrong. She just won't be driving it anytime soon."

"Why won't she?" he asked, not liking the sound of that.

She lifted one brow. "Did you not notice all her stuff is gone and your garage is now empty?"

He shook his head. "I didn't go home first.

"We moved all her stuff to a storage unit."

She had to be paying a lot per month for a unit that size. "I told her she could leave her stuff there until she found an apartment."

Amanda moved into the house. He followed her and closed the door behind him. When she turned back, he saw an expression he didn't like. "She left."

"Where did she go?" he asked, not liking the feeling of dread growing in his gut.

"She's in Hawaii. I dropped her at the airport yesterday."

"She visiting her parents?" he asked, knowing it was a shot in the dark to hope this was just a routine family visit and she'd be back in a week or two.

"Nope." She met his gaze. "She's moving back home. I convinced her not to ship all her stuff yet. To give it a few months before she decided."

Thank God his sister had convinced her to leave her stuff here for a while. It gave him some hope things would change. That she'd change her mind and come back.

"Why did she leave?" He knew she'd been thinking about it, but for the future. Like maybe months from now. Not this week.

"Lots of reasons." She tipped her head toward the

kitchen. "Come sit. I've got dinner on the stove."

For the first time he noticed the house smelled great as the aroma of cooking meat wafted to him.

"Stew?" he asked.

"Beef stroganoff," she corrected.

Though he felt like he'd been hit in the gut with a two-by-four and had lost all desire to eat when he'd heard Gabby was gone, his empty stomach had scented food nearby and was starting to wake up in a big way.

In the kitchen, Amanda gave the pot a stir, replaced the lid and adjusted the heat of the burner. Finally she turned back to him. "We ran the numbers on her last job. She didn't earn what she'd been hoping on it."

"So she can get another job." No big deal as far as he was concerned. Hell, she could probably earn a living turning trash into stuff to sell.

Amanda shook her head. "It wasn't just the money. I told her she could stay here for as long as she needed but she refused."

"Why now? She was already living here. Nothing's changed."

"Actually, something has." Amanda's hand dropped to her belly.

His gaze followed the move. The clues started to add up in his mind. Her refusing wine. Her having only one small cup of coffee the other morning when she was usually guzzling the stuff by the gallon.

His eyes grew wide. "You're . . ."

"Knocked up?" She smiled. "Yes, I am. You're going to be an uncle."

He moved around to his sister and wrapped her in a big hug. "That's really great, sis."

"Yes it is. Now you have to be nice to me because I'm pregnant."

He pulled back and scowled. "It figures you'd think of that."

But now Gabby moving out made sense. She didn't want to impose on her friend after the baby came.

But still, Amanda wasn't even showing yet. The baby was more than half a year away. So why did she pick up and run? He'd only been gone a damn week.

He shook his head. "I still don't know what the rush was. I mean last we talked she didn't mention any definite plans to move. Certainly not for this week."

"And when was the last time you talked?" Amanda crossed her arms and cocked up one brow.

His sister's aggressive stance put him immediately on the defense. "The last night of my leave. And you can just step back, sis. I know I haven't talked to her for a week and that's not my fault. You know what my job is like so you should have explained it to her and don't go blaming me for her taking off."

"I tried. I told her you must be busy. But it wasn't just last week."

"Then what was it?"

She shook her head. "So many things. You didn't even discuss what you were to each other."

"I was going to," he defended. It was why he'd come over. Or one of the reasons.

"When?"

"Tonight." That this was a recent decision just made today was something Amanda didn't need to know.

She drew in a breath. "Well, I guess you took too

long."

Exasperated, he threw up his hands. "I was away."

"I know." She sighed. "But you know what? Your job is not really a good excuse."

He opened his mouth to call bull shit on that but she didn't give him a chance to speak.

Bowling right over him, Amanda continued, "*Because* of how dangerous and demanding your job is, you should never wait to say or do anything. Every time you leave here, leave me, leave *her*, you should stop and make sure you've left nothing unsaid. Because you're right, we never know when or if you're ever coming back."

He couldn't argue. She was right.

"I thought it was too soon." It was his only defense.

"*You* knew what you were thinking, but she didn't. In her mind, you went dark for a whole week after you'd spent like two weeks together. She thinks you ghosted her. That she was just a fling."

"I never wanted her to be just a fling," he whispered, as much to himself as to Amanda.

That was the reason he'd avoided being with her for so long, until he realized the benefits of being with her outweighed the risks. And by benefits he wasn't talking sex—though that was damn nice too. He liked all of her.

He more than liked her.

"I know that," Amanda said. "But you need to tell her."

He nodded and turned for the door.

"You're going?" she called after him.

"Yeah." He stopped in his path, turned and strode back to give Amanda a goodbye hug. He hadn't been unaffected by what she'd said to him. "Congrats again on the baby."

Outside, Zach got into the truck and didn't wait. He pulled out is cell and dialed Gabby's number.

When she answered on the second ring, she sounded breathless.

"Hi," he said and then launched right into what she needed to know to feel better. "I was away and had no cell signal. That's why I didn't call. This is the first chance I had. I'm sorry."

She drew in a shaky breath loud enough he heard it clearly across the miles. "I'm glad you're back safely."

"It was just a training."

She laughed but the sound was far from amused. More judgmental, if possible. "Amanda told me you always say it's a training."

Amanda was an over-sharer, but it was good to hear Gabby laugh, even if he suspected it was sarcastically.

"This time it's true," he said, admitting what he probably shouldn't be to a girl who wasn't his girlfriend. At least, not yet.

"So, Hawaii, huh?"

"Yeah." After a short pause, she said, "The twin-sized bed in my old bedroom seems smaller than I remembered."

His heart broke for her when he heard the defeat in her voice.

"When are you coming back?" he asked, hopeful. If he was part of the reason she left, he could make it right.

"Why do you want to know?" The chill in her tone traveled just fine from Hawaii to his ear.

"Gabby, I know I should have clarified things before I went back on duty." He'd honestly thought that first day back would be a normal day and he'd be home by dinner.

But Amanda was right. After being in the Navy since he'd turned eighteen, he knew to expect the unexpected.

"I'm sorry I didn't say so before, but I want to keep seeing you." He realized that sounded too much like she'd be his booty call and nothing else.

That wasn't the case. Not at all.

Zach rushed to add, "And I want to go out to dinner and go trash hunting and do whatever else you want. I like spending time with you."

She let out a short laugh that seemed a little off. "Now you tell me?"

The shake in her voice told him she was most likely crying.

Dare he hope they were happy tears? "So when are you coming back?" he asked again.

"I'm not."

"Why not?" He knew the other thing that sent her running and said, "If you don't feel comfortable staying with Amanda after the baby comes, you can stay with me."

Jesus, this was moving fast. From no girlfriend to a live-in one, in the span of one conversation. He wasn't having heart palpitations at the idea, so that was good.

"I can't do that."

"Because . . ." he prompted.

"Because I'm a failure. I can't make a go of it as a designer. I can't make a living wage in California and I'm not going to sponge off my friends."

Friends. Meaning both him and Amanda?

He'd made the leap to them being friends to being in a relationship but apparently she hadn't. And maybe she was right.

Rushing into things too fast rather than building slowly might be the sure way to sink them when they've just begun.

But still, Hawaii?

Shit. That was far. Too far.

He could get permission from command to fly there occasionally, but not often enough.

He'd just have to fly her to see him, if she was willing. At this point, he wasn't sure.

"Gabby, if you want to be with me, we'll make it work. We'll make *us* work, even with an ocean between us."

Long distance would suck but he'd do it. For her.

Besides, he was away a lot too. If he was in Djibouti, it didn't matter if she was in California or Hawaii.

He could do this. They could do this together . . . if she wanted to.

She drew in a breath as he waited. Finally, she said, "Okay."

"Okay?" He jumped on the answer.

"Yeah. But can you try to be a little more communicative when you're able to?" She let out a sigh. "It's been a really long week."

He heard the weariness in her voice and felt the guilt again. "I will. I promise."

Hell, he'd get a sat phone if he had to, just to keep in touch with her while it was somewhere without cell service.

It was hard to believe. He hadn't wanted a

girlfriend. Then he had. And now she was in Hawaii. Shit timing all around. But they'd make it work.

They had to, because now he'd had her in his life, he couldn't imagine life without her.

CHAPTER TWENTY-FOUR

"Have you talked to Gabby recently?" Amanda asked in a tone so like their mother Zach couldn't help but tease her about it.

"Yes, mother," he joked. "Not that it's any of your business, but we talk every night."

After a week, he and Gabby had settled into a routine. The moment he got home from base, he'd get on the computer and they'd get on video chat.

The phone was ruined for him forever. Hearing her voice was nice, but seeing her smile was so much better.

But dating his sister's friend was proving to be a challenge since Amanda thought she had the right to be involved in everything now.

Bringing his sister to McP's for lunch was proving to be another challenge.

If she continued to glare at him like she was now, no doubt because of his comparing her to their mother, she was going to ruin even his favorite bar for him.

"Well, I'm glad you're at least keeping in touch,"

she said. "Now if you could convince her to move back here we could all be happy. I miss her."

He missed her too. He pressed his lips together to keep in the words. Talking about feelings with his sister was right up there with talking about sex with her.

"You're the accountant. Can't you figure out a way for her to turn a profit on her business?"

"Believe me. I'm trying." Amanda ran a finger down the condensation of her glass of ice water with lemon.

Beer in hand, Zach watched her and thought once again how grateful he was that it was the females who had to stop drinking during pregnancy, not the males of the species.

Selfish, maybe, but true.

"I've helped her as much as I could already. Or as much as she'd let me. I even signed her up for an affiliate account and added the code to her blog so she'd earn some money from her web traffic."

Most of that went right over Zach's head but he got the gist. Amanda was trying to help but it still wasn't enough.

"Thanks for trying," he said.

"I'm not giving up yet. I recommend her to everyone who might possibly need a designer." She let out a short laugh. "I even entered her into a design competition. I figured she'd forgive me for doing it behind her back if she wins."

"How did you enter her without her knowing?"

"Easy. I just filled out the application pretending I was her. I had plenty of pictures of her projects between what was on her blog and what pictures I could take from my house and your house."

"My house?" His eyes widened.

"Yup."

"You snuck in while I was away again?" he asked.

"Yup." She looked too happy with herself. "That shutter headboard looks amazing, by the way."

He scowled. "I'm going to need my spare key back."

"Nope." she said sweetly. "And if she wins and moves back, you'll be thanking me for sneaking in."

He hated when she was right. "I don't want to admit it, but sometimes I do enjoy how sneaky you are. Not all the time, but sometimes."

"Thanks." She beamed at what most people wouldn't consider exactly a compliment.

Maybe he could rent Gabby a storefront and sell some of the things she'd made for his house to prove to her she had a marketable skill. But he didn't think he'd be able to part with anything. She'd created everything just for him. Every item held memories of her.

Zach was still racking his brain, trying to figure out how to get Gabby back to the mainland, when Amanda gasped.

"What's wrong?" Zach took in the area around them, looking for the threat before he focused back on his sister. "Are you in pain? Is it the baby?"

"Shh. No. It's Clay and Tasha," she hissed.

"Clay and who?" he asked, obviously too loudly for her taste as she shushed him again, her eyes impossibly wide.

She leaned forward. "Clay and Tasha from *Hot House*."

"I don't know what hot house is." He kept his voice down this time so she didn't have an aneurism and hurt herself or his unborn niece or nephew.

"It's a reality show about home renovation."

"Oh, one of those." Less interested now, he leaned back and grabbed his beer.

"Would it impress you more if I told you Clay's a retired SEAL."

"Not really." Even so, Zach let his gaze wander over to the table off the side that Amanda kept staring at.

"Don't look!" she squeaked.

He let out a laugh. "As if they haven't noticed you looking?"

"That's different. I'm a fan. I love that show. Gabby and I used to watch it together—" Amanda's sentence trailed off as did her attention. There was a faraway look in her narrowed eyes as she said, "Hmm."

"Hmm, what?" He hated to even ask what crazy idea she had, but he did anyway.

He knew that look. She'd gotten it when she'd decided it would be legal if she drove with her learner's permit if he, at seventeen but with a senior license, was in the car with her. Their parents had other ideas about that and, of course, he'd gotten the brunt of that punishment and couldn't drive for a month.

She'd also gotten that look when she and Gabby got the bright idea to make s'mores on the gas stove in the kitchen one college break while their parents were out. They'd almost set the place on fire. Lucky for them he'd been home that weekend and knew how to work a fire extinguisher.

He could only hope that Amanda's idea now was better than her past brainstorms.

HOT SEAL, TIJUANA NIGHTS

She planted her hands on the edge of the table and pushed her chair back. "I'm going to talk to them."

He groaned. "Please don't."

No doubt she was going to drag him into this. Probably try to play the *my brother's a SEAL too* card with this Clay dude so they'd listen to her.

Before he could beg her some more she was across McP's courtyard and standing next to the table where a man and woman sat trying to enjoy a private meal together.

With a sigh, he pushed his own chair back, shoved his hands in his pockets and reluctantly moved to stand behind Amanda.

He tipped his head to the strangers. "Please forgive my sister. She's easily excited."

"That's all right. We're always happy to speak with fans." The woman smiled sweetly, looking genuinely happy to talk to them.

The dude, not so much. Zach felt his pain.

"So I love the show and I love your story. How the two of you met working on the show and fell in love," Amanda said. "It's all so romantic."

Clay let out a snort while Tasha patted his hand as she smiled at Amanda. "Thank you. We think so."

"Anyway, the reason I'm here—my friend, his girlfriend too actually—is a decorator. And what she does is pretty amazing. Really unique stuff. Right, Zach?" Amanda looked back at him.

"Well, she snuck in while I was deployed and redecorated my house with shit she found in the trash and I don't hate it, so yeah, I'd say that's amazing."

For the first time the dude cracked a smile.

"You at Coronado?" he asked Zach.

"Yeah. Team 3. You?" Zach asked.

"Team 1. Retired now," Clay answered.

Zach tipped his head to acknowledge a fellow frogman.

Meanwhile the women were still talking. He paid more attention and noticed Amanda handing Tasha a business card, before she wrapped her arms around the woman in a hug too big for a stranger.

He caught the amused expression on Clay's face and said, "Sorry about this."

Clay lifted a shoulder. "Happens all the time. I'm getting used to it."

His comment made Zach feel moderately better about the intrusion.

Finally—thankfully—Amanda said, "Thank you both again, so much. Come on, Zach. Let's let them enjoy their meal."

As if *he'd* been the one stopping them from doing that?

His brows shot high but he said his good-byes and followed Amanda back to their table.

"You want to tell me what that was about?" he asked.

"Yes, but I'm afraid I'll jinx it."

"Fine." He reached for his beer and waited. He knew his sister. She couldn't keep a secret for shit.

Amanda didn't disappoint. She huffed out a breath and leaned forward. "Okay. I can tell you this. If it works out, we'll both get Gabby back."

"All right then." He nodded and lifted his bottle in salute. "Here's to your crazy ideas."

He'd probably lost his mind, believing this one could actually work, but he hoped it would with everything he had in him.

CHAPTER TWENTY-FIVE

"Gabrielle, clean up. It's time for dinner."

She sighed and itched her nose with the back of her hand, careful not to get paint on her face.

"Five more minutes," she called back.

It wasn't lost on her she might as well have been a teenager again. Sleeping in her old room. Having dinner at five p.m. because that's when her father liked to eat. Making her bed first thing every morning so her mother didn't have to *remind* her to do it.

Worse, she felt like a teenager again. Amanda had a grown up job, a house, a husband and a baby on the way. Zach too, with his own house and his kick ass job, was busy adulting, and defending the country from evil.

And here she was. Jobless. Aimless.

For the past month the only thing keeping her sane was her blog. She'd gone in full force, posting daily plus recycling old posts on social media.

She'd taken over the back of the garage and had about five projects, all in various stages of completion, going at one time and she blogged about it all. She'd even gotten quite a nice following on IGTV.

Too bad blogging didn't pay better. If it did she'd be set. As it was, the couple of hundred dollars or so she got a month from the affiliate account Amanda had insisted she get wasn't going to cut it.

It was enough to pay her cell phone bill, her storage unit rental back in California and buy chalk paint for her projects, but it wouldn't cover rent on her own place.

She'd be stuck here in her parents' house forever.

"Gabby!" her mother shouted again.

"I said I'm coming. I just have to finish this—"

The door between the kitchen and the garage opening cut off what might have become a full-blown rant worthy of a teenage girl.

"You have a phone call," her mother said.

"Oh." She pocketed the guilt and the annoyance and struggled to stand. "Thanks."

Setting down the paintbrush on the edge of the can, she followed her mother back into the kitchen and spotted the cordless phone on the counter.

She did her best to ignore the course catalog also on the counter. Her father was trying to talk her into going back to school to be *something useful.*

He'd suggested an accountant like Amanda since, according to him, *everyone needs their taxes done.*

Kill her now.

She loved Amanda. Loved her as much as she would hate being an accountant.

Shoving the catalog into the junk drawer, she picked up the phone. It had to be Amanda. No one else she knew even had the number for her parents' landline.

"Hello?"

"Is this Gabrielle Lee?"

"Uh, yes. Who's this?"

"I'm Mary Ross. I work for New Millennia Media."

"Okay." Was this some sort of survey or something?

"I'm happy to inform you, you've won the Hot House Design Competition through THN—The Home Nation Station."

"I what?"

"Yes! I know it's a surprise but you won. I was wondering about your availability. We're hoping you can come here to the studio in San Diego so we can film you receiving the prize."

What the hell? "Um, could you remind me what the prize is again?"

"Ten-thousand dollars. And of course the photo op will be great publicity for your design business. We'll have your story and your contact info on our website for the duration of the year."

Gabby was having trouble absorbing what else Mary was saying. Hell, she'd nearly dropped the phone. Everything after the words *ten-thousand dollars* got kind of lost amid the buzzing in her head.

"So can you get here? Where am I calling you, anyway?"

"Uh, Hawaii. My parents live here."

"Nice. I'm jealous." Mary laughed. "We can book you a flight. Are you free this week?"

"Yeah. Free. Completely. Yes. Thank you." She couldn't get enough words out to accept.

"Perfect. Text me which airport you'd like to leave from and I'll book the ticket and send you the flight details. Check your email for the confirmation. And congratulations!"

"Thank you." Gabby disconnected and stared at her mother and father, already seated at the kitchen table eating.

"Who was that?" her mother asked.

"The Home Nation channel. I won their design competition."

Even her father looked up from his poi at her announcement.

"I didn't know you'd entered a competition," her mother said.

Still in a daze, Gabby said, "Neither did I."

But she had her suspicions about who did know. She reached for her cell phone, plugged into the wall.

That earned her a glare from her mother. "Gabby. No calls. It's time for dinner."

Lips pressed tight, she set down her phone. She reviewed the call with Mary, focusing on the good things. Ten-thousand dollars. A flight to San Diego. Her business featured on their website.

It was enough to have her manage even a small smile as she said, "Yes, Mama."

CHAPTER TWENTY-SIX

Gabby walked the long hallway past the gates and finally, out into the Arrivals area of San Diego International.

Her carry-on in tow, she paused and glanced around.

She'd asked Amanda to pick her up at the airport, but it was Zach's head she spotted above those waiting. Her heart fluttered.

Her boyfriend had met her at the airport. It made her want to turn to the travelers nearby and say, *That's my boyfriend. He's here to get me.*

She didn't, but she did walk as fast as humanly possible while towing her crappy, wonky-wheeled overstuffed bag behind her.

Smiling, he took a step forward and met her. Then the bag was abandoned and the other travelers forgotten as he lifted her with two hands around her waist.

In the middle of the terminal, she wrapped her legs around his waist and kissed him hard. She shaking by the time he put her down on the ground.

"I missed you," he said.

Fighting the mist of tears, she said, "I missed you too."

"You have a checked bag?" He tipped his head toward the luggage carousels.

"Nope. Just this." She spun to make sure her bag was still where she'd left it, ignored and unattended as she'd jumped Zach.

He reached for the handle. "Good girl. I didn't want to wait." He grinned.

Gabby nodded. "Yeah. We'd better get to Amanda's. I bet she's losing her mind waiting for us."

"Probably. She wanted to come to the airport, but I wouldn't let her."

"Why not?" Gabby asked.

"I wanted time alone with you. It's been over a month." He widened his eyes as if that amount of time apart was unimaginable.

The intensity in his gaze—and the bulge in his jeans—told her what he had been missing most during that month and she nearly laughed.

She'd dreamed of having Zach be hers—what she hadn't thought about was what the care and feeding of a man like Zach entailed. Apparently, certain needs came first, above all else.

Gabby could live with that. She was feeling pretty needy herself.

"Quick stop at your house first on the way to Amanda's?" she asked.

"Mmm, hmm," he said, stopping to lean low. "That's what I was hoping for."

He squeezed her arm with his free hand and pressed a quick kiss to her mouth.

"Or maybe not so quick of a stop," he added.

She laughed. "Okay."

Zach broke a few laws getting from the airport to his house. She held on to the roof handle and didn't complain.

She'd been missing him too and the couple of times she'd even considered video or phone sex with him, her mother had come knocking on her door with laundry or for something else. They'd both been deprived.

That was more than obvious from the trail of clothes that led from Zach's front door to the bedroom. They were both naked by the time they collapsed on his bed.

There was no foreplay. No talking. Just Zach covering himself and groaning against her neck as he plunged inside her.

She had no complaints. It felt amazing to have him so desperate for her.

He felt amazing as he pushed inside her.

She tipped her hips up and he plunged deeper, hitting just the right spot to have her breath coming faster.

He pounded her into one orgasm and kept going as the second hit her. Zach joined her for that one, then, while she was still quaking with aftershocks, he changed condoms and came back for round two.

She loved when he did that. She loved him.

He stopped thrusting and, still as a statue, he looked down at her, his gaze on hers. "I love you too."

Shit. Her eyes opened wide as she reviewed the past minute. "I said that out loud?"

"Yeah, you did." He smiled.

She couldn't feel too bad about the slip because

he'd said it back.

He loved her.

Her heart felt like it was exploding. Swelling so big it would outgrow its place in her chest.

He started moving inside her again. Slowly, deeply, all while his eyes never left hers.

It felt different. They were different.

And holy hell, sex was so much more amazing now. How could one little four-letter word change so much?

She didn't know, but she liked it.

And wow, she really liked what he was doing to her as he lifted her hips higher and nudged that spot that had her spine tingling.

He added a thumb on her clit and she exploded one more time.

He held out until she was exhausted before he flipped her over onto her belly and pounded himself to completion before collapsing over her back, panting.

She felt Zach smiling where his cheek pressed against her and asked, "What?"

He lifted one shoulder and rolled off her. She snuggled against him and nestled in the crook of his neck, as he said, "I'm just happy you're here. And happy you won."

"Won the contest that I didn't know I entered, you mean?" she asked.

"That's Amanda for you. Don't act surprised."

"I'm not. But I am grateful, even if she did overstep."

"Ten-thousand dollars is a nice payoff for her butting her nose in your business," he pointed out.

"For sure. Ten-thousand dollars is great. Huge.

But it's not even six month's living expenses here in California. Between rent and internet and food and electric." She'd been doing a lot of number crunching lately.

Gabby had learned her lesson after the shop job. Everything had to be laid out on spreadsheets, whether she liked it or not.

"Let's not talk about this now." It was spoiling her post-orgasm bliss.

"No. I want to talk about it." Zach sat up a bit higher against the pillows, increasing the distraction of his bare chest. "Don't pay rent. Move in with me."

It took her a second to absorb what he'd just said. He'd said she could stay with him before, after she'd found out Amanda was pregnant, but this seemed different.

Temporarily staying at his place and moving in together were two very different things.

"You want to live together?" she asked.

"Yes." He said it with no doubt. Like the decision was logical. Easy.

With his strong arms wrapped around her, it felt possible.

But she had to think with her head, not her heart . . . or parts lower.

"You're not afraid it's too soon?" she asked.

"No." Again, there wasn't even a shadow of a doubt in his voice.

She should have realized when Zach did something he went all in. After such a glacially slow start, she'd just never imagined the thing he'd rush head on into would be their relationship.

It was so new she still pinched herself each morning to make sure it wasn't a dream. She still waited daily for it all to implode.

But he was so brave. He made her want to be that way too.

She bit her lip, wanting with everything in her to say yes. But she was afraid.

What if it didn't work? What if having her in his house, underfoot all the time, made him realize that all the things that had annoyed him about her for all those years still did?

What if he realized he was right all along and she was just a big pain in his butt?

"Come on, Gabby. Say yes." Those eyes, as deep as the ocean and just as intense, locked onto hers. Those lips, so tempting. Those muscles, holding her in his embrace. It all made it hard to resist his request.

"Maybe. I'll think about it. Okay?"

One brow cocked high. "You'll think about it?" He let out a laugh, as if he couldn't believe she hadn't said yes.

Apparently Zach wasn't good at not getting his way. It was kind of entertaining.

Finally, he said with amusement in his voice, "All right."

Aloud he'd agreed, but she had a feeling that in his head he was already planning his strategy.

He was a SEAL after all. They were aggressive problem solvers, as far as she could see. He'd probably have her moving in with him by week's end.

She couldn't wait to see the creative ways he came up with to convince her.

When Zach looked like he was about to start his campaign right then, probably with a few more orgasms to sway her decision, she swung her feet to the floor and hopped away from the bed and out of his reach.

"We have to get going."

He scowled. "Okay. But we'll be continuing this later."

She certainly hoped so.

They finally made it to Amanda's house. As they stood outside the door, Zach shot her a glance. "Remember, your plane just landed and we came straight here. We did not go to my place first. Got it?"

Gabby was more concerned with how good dinner smelled. Jasper must be grilling something out back. Burgers, maybe? Whatever it was was more interesting than Zach's worry about his sister.

"You need to stop lying to Amanda. And you really need to stop trying to drag me into it. Remember, I was her friend before I was your girlfriend."

"Fine." His pout had her laughing as she stood on tiptoe to kiss the expression off his lips.

"Ugh. Get a room, you two," Amanda said as she opened the door and saw them.

"Gladly." Zach reached for her hand.

"Stop." Gabby tugged it away and hugged Amanda. "It's so good to see you. I missed you."

"Then move back," Amanda said, with a good bit of attitude as she squeezed Gabby in a hug.

Gabby rolled her eyes at the siblings multipronged attack to get her back here and walked past Amanda into the house.

"Whatever's cooking smells—" She didn't get to finish the sentence as her cell phone rang, loud and obnoxious, in the back pocket of her jeans. "Ugh, who's calling?"

One glance at the screen had her eyes widening.

"It's the studio," she told the room at large. She rushed to answer in her professional voice, "Hello, this is Gabrielle Lee."

She didn't miss Amanda's raised brow and Zach's chuckle at her new formal greeting.

"Hi, it's Mary. Just checking you landed safely and are still good with tomorrow's shoot."

"Yup. Everything is fine. I'll be at the studio tomorrow."

"Great. But that's not the only reason I'm calling. We had a production meeting today with Tasha Jones. She's the—"

Gabby gasped. "The host of *Hot House*."

"Yes. I see you're familiar with the show."

"Definitely."

"Well, Tasha had an interesting idea. She wanted you to be a guest on the show this season. Come in for one episode. Take her and Clay dumpster diving then bring the finds back to the Imperial Beach house for upcycling. Are you interested?"

"Oh my God. Yes, I'm interested."

"Okay. Great. So we'll talk details tomorrow after the photo shoot."

"Yes. Thank you."

After Mary said goodbye and disconnected Gabby stood there with the cell in her hand unable to move or form a sentence until Zach squeezed her arm.

"You okay?"

"Yes." She laughed, gathering herself enough to tell them the good news. "The network wants me to take Tasha and Clay dumpster diving on the show."

"Oh my God!" Amanda rushed forward.

Zach shook his head. "Oh, Clay's going to love that." The sarcasm was clear in his voice.

"I know! He'll hate it. That's why it's so perfect! That's why I suggested it." Amanda grinned.

"You suggested it?" Gabby's eyes widened.

Amanda bit her lip. "We ran into Clay and Tasha at McP's."

"And Amanda marched right up to the table and attacked them in the middle of their meal. I didn't realize why then, but I do now." Zach folded his arms.

"And it worked. See?" Amanda challenged.

Zach smiled. "Yes. Apparently it did."

Still in a daze, from so many things, Gabby's head spun.

Going on *Hot House* could make her a household name. It could bring in a ton of business. Jobs she couldn't take if she wasn't in California.

She wasn't willing to give up on her dream. Not when things were finally going her way. And she didn't want to be away from Zach any longer. Not now that they'd admitted they were in love.

She turned to Zach. "Yes."

"Yes, what?" he asked.

"Yes, I'll move in with you."

His smile was blocked from view as Amanda body slammed her with a big hug. "Yay!"

Gabby laughed and caught Zach's gaze. He smiled and her heart swelled.

Yay just about covered how she felt too.

EPILOGUE

"You're really going to do it?" Nitro asked.

"I really am." Zach nodded and downed the last of his beer.

"I wish you luck, bro." Justus extended a hand to Zach.

He hoped he wouldn't need it, but Zach accepted his teammate's well wishes and tossed a bill on the bar.

"Text and let us know what she says," Nitro called at his back.

"Will do," Zach waved as he pushed through the exit at McP's and out to the street.

He knew a couple of the guys thought he was nuts. It hadn't even been a year since the night he'd come home from Djibouti and found her—an uninvited guest—in his shower.

But he was ready.

When he'd come home from that week of training and had found her gone he'd realized he didn't want to ever feel that way again.

It was like death by a thousand cuts from a

thousand memories of her there. The salt in the wound the realization she wasn't there anymore.

He wasn't going to go through that again.

And so he was going to drive to the house—their house—with a ring in his pocket and not one doubt in his mind.

Unless she wasn't home.

Shit. He should find out first. She'd been working late a lot.

He punched in a text.

Where are you?

Her reply came back.

Office.

He swung the truck around and headed in the opposite direction, to Gabby's new office. She needed an official office now that she had a new job.

A lot had changed.

He drove up to the storefront and pulled behind the production van parked out front.

The crew was with Gabby more than he was. He'd made it clear early on they'd better keep him off camera—or risk their very expensive equipment.

They'd been co-existing peacefully in Gabby's life—so far.

The cameraman greeted Zach with a tip of his chin. He got a wave from the director and a smile from her assistant.

It had been an education for him, getting to know the ins and out of cable television and reality show production—whether he'd wanted to know it or not.

He stayed in the background, hanging out behind the camera until finally the chick in charge called it a wrap for the day because, thank God, this wasn't one of those twenty-four hour a day kind of shows.

Gabby caught a glimpse of him and smiled.

She put down the rubber tire she was holding—why she was holding it, he had no clue—and came toward him.

"Hey." She rose on her toes and pressed both palms to his chest.

"Hey, back." He dipped his head to meet her halfway for a quick kiss. "You doing some auto mechanic stuff now?" he joked.

"No. The tire is going to be a decorative planter for the front lawn."

He eyed the old dirty rubber tire.

"*Our* front lawn?" he asked, cringing at the thought.

"No. It's for a job. But if you don't stop being judgmental before you even see the finished product, I'll make a whole bunch for our house, so stop."

"I will reserve judgment. I swear." His lips twitched at how fierce she got over her projects. "It's a shame you're all done for the day and I won't be treated to any more live *Trash to Treasure* action."

She narrowed her eyes at him. "Somehow, I doubt you're really all that disappointed." She shook her head. "I still can't believe this is my life now. I have my own show on television. Or at least it will be when it airs next month."

"Believe it. It's all true, so you'd better get used to it." He bracketed her in his arms with one hand on each of her hips.

"I'll try," she said, her hands still resting on his pecs, which even after all these months together she still seemed to be obsessed with.

She was adorable. Every little thing she did and said made him happy. Just thinking of her had him smiling.

He'd been planning to wait. Maybe take her out to dinner. Or do it at home over champagne and chocolate covered strawberries, or something else corny and expected. But the time felt right now.

She was happy. So comfortable in her element in the space she'd created for herself. He couldn't wait.

Zach reached into his pocket. "There's something else you're going to have to get used to."

Her eyes widened as she glanced down at his open palm.

There was a, "Holy shit," from somewhere behind him before a bunch of rustling and then the crew went silent.

Zach ignored them and forged ahead. He dropped down to one knee and gazed up at the dark-haired beauty he was lucky enough to call his.

"Gabrielle Lee, it feels like I've known you forever, but then again, I know I didn't really start to know you at all until that first night I heard you singing Disney songs in my shower. And now I know I never want to be without you."

He grasped the ring between his thumb and forefinger and held it up. A bright light coming from behind him reflected off the diamond and Zach had a strong suspicion his days of being off camera had ended.

Ignoring that the director was no doubt hoping their private moment would end up on TV, he decided to deal with that issue later and finish what he started.

"Gabby, will you marry me?"

Tears filled her eyes as she nodded. "Oh my God. Yes."

When he slipped the ring on her finger the applause from the crew was one more reminder they weren't alone, not even close, but he couldn't care.

He was on his feet and kissing his new fiancé and it felt damn good.

The chick in charge already had her cell phone out. "Hey, I've got a pitch for you. Gabby and Zach are getting married. How about a DIY Your Wedding show?"

Zach let out a sigh. He glanced down at Gabby, who was smiling through her tears.

"We don't have to do anything you don't want to. Hell, we can elope if you want," she said.

He shook his head. "I want you to have the wedding you want to have. Even if it means—God help me—dumpster diving behind the Home Depot for wood to build the altar."

"Really?" Her face glowed with happiness.

He understood the tired but indulgent expression on Clay's face at McP's now more than ever. "Really."

Maybe he and Clay needed to start a support group.

"Gabby." The director was suddenly next to them, cell still in hand and poised near her ear. "Can we start brainstorming wedding stuff this week and do some preliminary filming next Monday so we have something to show for the pitch?"

Gabby shot Zach a questioning glance. He nodded. "Yeah, sure. Go ahead. Next week is perfect actually."

The team was scheduled to go wheels up Sunday night. He'd be nowhere nearby and would miss the whole thing. Excellent.

He'd figure out how to get through this. They'd

figure it out together. Gabby was worth that and so much more.

"Oh my God. I just had a brilliant idea. What if *everything* for the wedding was upcycled? Not just the decorations but like everything. Right down to the dresses and the gifts from the guests." The production assistant was nearly vibrating with excitement over her idea.

The director's eyes widened. "I love it!"

Zach was afraid to ask, but he did anyway. "Upcycled means like using stuff you find in the trash, doesn't it?"

Gabby cringed. "Pretty much."

He pressed his lips together and nodded. Yup, this was going to get interesting.

"I love you," Gabby whispered. He didn't miss the little tinge of doubt in her tone.

That insecure shit was going to stop. He never wanted his woman to ever doubt what she meant to him. That he'd walk through fire for her.

Hell, he was even willing to have a dumpster wedding for her.

He pressed her face between his palms and said, "And I love you. Always. Never forget that." He kissed her hard and deep enough to make sure she believed it.

When he broke the kiss it was to see the camera right there in their faces, barely a foot away. He leveled a glare on the lens since he couldn't see the man behind it, before he turned his face toward Gabby.

"Can we go home now?" he asked.

She smiled. "Yes. Unless you want to stop by Amanda's so I can show her the ring—"

"Later."

Much later.

In fact, tomorrow sounded good to him. He had plans for tonight. He grabbed her hand and pulled her out of the studio.

He called back, "You guys can lock up, right?"

"You got it, big guy!" the director said, before continuing, "Keep filming until they drive out of sight."

"Jesus." He shook his head.

"You regretting asking me to marry you?" Gabby asked.

He paused on the way to the truck to haul her against him and shook his head. "Never."

"Hey, you know what I'd like to do?" she asked.

The possibilities were endless and tantalizing. "No, what?"

"I want to go back to Tijuana."

His eyes widened. "Not for more tile—"

She shook her head. "No. Not for more tile. For us. I saw some nice-looking hotels and restaurants that night we were there. It would be fun to spend a night or a couple there. You know, when we're not on the run from a drug cartel."

He wouldn't mind a few nights in Tijuana with the woman he loved, but he'd assumed she'd be afraid. "I thought you'd never want to go back there again after last time."

Her gaze met and held his. "Why not? I'll go anywhere with you."

Even after all this time, when she said things like that her blind faith in him nearly brought him to his knees.

He cleared the emotion from his throat and said,

"I'll talk to command and see if I can get approved for a couple of days leave."

"That'd be great. But do that tomorrow." The need in her gaze told him they had more important things to do tonight.

Zach pulled her closer. "Tomorrow."

Dear Reader,

I hope you enjoyed reading Zach and Gabby's story. But did you know the other SEALs you met have their own stories? Zach's teammates all get their happily-ever-afters in the SEALs in Paradise series of standalone novels.

You can read about Zane Alexander's exploits while he was a SEAL and after, in my Hot SEALs series titles SAVED BY A SEAL and SEAL THE DEAL.

Silas Branson's book is SEAL STRONG, part of the Silver SEALs series of standalone novels.

And last but not least, read Clay and Tasha's story in HOT SEAL, DIRTY MARTINI, also part of the SEALs in Paradise series.

Happy Reading!

XOXO
Cat Johnson

SEALS IN PARADISE

SEASON 1
Hot SEAL, Salty Dog Elle James
Hot SEAL, S*x on the Beach Delilah Devlin
Hot SEAL, Dirty Martini Cat Johnson
Hot SEAL, Bourbon Neat Parker Kincade
Hot SEAL, Red Wine Becca Jameson
Hot SEAL, Cold Beer Cynthia D'Alba
Hot SEAL, Rusty Nail Teresa Reasor
Hot SEAL, Black Coffee Cynthia D'Alba
Hot SEAL, Single Malt Kris Michaels

SEASON 2
Hot SEAL, Tijuana Nights Cat Johnson (Zach)
Hot SEAL, Hawaiian Nights Elle James (Hawk)
Hot SEAL, Savannah Nights Kris Michaels (Compass)
Hot SEAL, Vegas Nights Parker Kincade (Rocket)
Hot SEAL, Australian Nights Becca Jameson (Justus)
Hot SEAL, Roman Nights Teresa Reasor (Nitro)
Hot SEAL, New Orleans Nights Delilah Devlin (T-Bone)
Hot SEAL, Alaskan Nights Cynthia D'Alba (Dutch)

ABOUT THE AUTHOR

A top 10 *New York Times* bestselling author, Cat Johnson writes the *USA Today* bestselling Hot SEALs series, as well as contemporary romance featuring sexy alpha heroes who often wear cowboy or combat boots. Known for her creative marketing, Cat has sponsored bull-riding cowboys, used bologna to promote her romance novels, and owns a collection of camouflage and cowboy boots for book signings. She writes both full length and shorter works.

For more visit CatJohnson.net
Join the mailing list at catjohnson.net/news

Made in the USA
San Bernardino, CA
10 June 2019